A Saltwater Christmas

A Saltwater Christmas

Laurie Beach

Laurie Beach

A Saltwater Christmas
Copyright© 2024 Laurie Beach
Tule Publishing First Printing, November 2024

The Tule Publishing, Inc.

ALL RIGHTS RESERVED

First Publication by Tule Publishing 2024

No part of this book may be used or reproduced in any manner whatsoever without written permission except in the case of brief quotations embodied in critical articles and reviews.

This is a work of fiction. Names, characters, places, and incidents are products of the author's imagination or are used fictitiously. Any resemblance to actual events, locales, organizations, or persons, living or dead, is entirely coincidental.

ISBN: 978-1-965640-87-6

Dedication

For my sister, Susie Herring, with love and gratitude for continuing the family Christmas traditions.

Dear Reader,

I hope this story adds another good thing to your life: a moment of laughter, a new thought, or, at best, that feeling we get when we fall in love. Even though this is a work of fiction, it is your mind that brings this book to life, and your imagination that makes the characters real. I hope the people of Goose Island become your friends and this tale lifts your Christmas spirit.

My goal is always to provide a satisfying ending. Maybe not a perfect one, but a conclusion that makes you sigh with happiness and feel like the story wasn't a waste of your time. All of my books are designed with that in mind because life is hard enough sometimes. It's nice to have an escape, and getting away to the Christmas season is especially magical.

This novella kicks off my new *Southern Isles* series. Four more books are coming soon, beginning with *The Dogwood Days of Summer*.

I love to hear what my readers would like to see in future books. Please reach out to me through my website at www.lauriebeach.com. Also, let's be friends on social media! You can find me on Facebook as Laurie Beach, and on Instagram, TikTok, and Threads @beachauthor.

With love and gratitude,
Laurie Beach

Chapter One

ALLIE WESTLEY REFUSED to believe impossible things. Coincidences were just coincidences, unexplainable phenomena were merely things that lacked verifiable facts, aliens did not exist, and gut instincts were merely your subconscious taking in veiled clues. How anyone ever believed in Santa Claus was beyond her. Even as a three-year-old, she knew the truth. Christmas was just a guilt-inducing holiday that forced people to spend time with family they'd rather not be around. Her mother and her new boyfriend, in particular. There would be no candy canes, Christmas trees, red sweaters, eggnog, gingerbread, or gifts this year. Christmas was to be spent on the beach alone eating a ham and pickle sandwich in honor of her father. And then, maybe a nap.

Allie's job was starting in two days, and her new roommate, Sam Clare, was scheduled to move in that afternoon. She sat up in bed and took several deep, cleansing breaths. According to Sam's profile, she was supposed to be quiet and clean. Allie hoped that was true. Sam also came with a dog, but Allie was looking forward to that. Access to a pet without having to pay for vet bills was fine with her. And Buttercup the dog sounded cute.

Allie tapped the floor with her right big toe three times before she got out of bed, then straightened the sheets and comforter before the messiness caused her anxiety to sky-rocket. By the time she was out of the shower, she was excited to get the day started. Maybe she and Sam could do some shopping in Charleston for colorful pillows or something pretty to jazz up their shared space. Her big white couch fit in the family room perfectly, but some down-filled pillows to go with her hand-tufted Persian rug would add to the coziness. She wound her long auburn hair into her special ultra-absorbent towel and wrapped a bath sheet around her body before walking out into the hallway.

"Allison?"

She nearly lost both her towel and her footing at the sound of a deep male voice. She spun around to see a tall, muscular man standing at the end of the hallway. Like a possum, she froze. Thankfully, he wasn't moving toward her. He just stood there holding a can of Red Bull with a strange little smile on his face.

"I'm Sam," he said.

"What?" Her voice was oddly high-pitched. "You're not Sam. Sam is a girl."

"My mother will be shocked to hear that," he joked.

"I asked for a female roommate."

"Then one of us clicked the wrong button."

Clearly, he'd been the one to make the mistake. Probably on purpose. Allie would never mess up like that. She pulled at her towel to make sure all of the important parts were covered. "Well, you need to unclick it and find some other place. I am not living with a man."

"I already paid my portion of the deposit," he said.

The unworried smirk on his face made her want to kick him. "So did I," she spat back. "And I paid mine first."

He turned and walked toward the kitchen like he'd been living there all his life. "I guess we're gonna have to make the best of it."

"No." Her voice rose as she clutched her towel tightly at her chest. "I was here first. You need to leave. We'll work out the deposit thing with the landlord."

"If you don't want to live with me, then I'm happy to help you clear out your stuff."

He spoke in the most smug, obstinate way, and if she weren't wearing only a towel, she would have physically forced him out. He was twice her size and at least a foot taller, but in that moment, she didn't care.

He placed his Red Bull on her pristine mahogany console table and picked up a moving box, then forced her to press herself against the wall as he walked past her to the empty bedroom across the hall. "I just put some fried chicken in the fridge if you want some." He threw the words at her like he was the nicest guy on the planet and she was the one with the problem.

Was he trying to ply her with chicken? She fumed. "Don't touch my groceries," she said, finally able to move again. "I know exactly how many kombuchas I have in there." She stormed into her bedroom.

"Gut problems?" he asked like the interfering jerk he was.

"No. Roommate problems." She slammed her door and leaned against it, breathing heavily. She'd been so looking forward to her new friend Sam Clare—to nights drinking wine, having girl talk, and watching reality television. It had been a mistake to agree to live with someone she'd never met—never even *seen*. Sam Clare had no presence on social media. The picture he'd included with his application was of an entire family. She'd assumed he was one of the girls. How had she been so stupid? The only things she'd asked in their brief text introductions were where he was coming from and what kind of dog he had. *Montana*, he'd said. And, *a well-trained mutt*.

She changed as quickly as she could into her matching cream knit set in case he kicked her door down or peeked in through a crack or something. Her heart thumped with disappointment and fury. She had no intention of living with a man. Her mother would be horrified. Allie brushed out her hair and tied it into a wet bun on top of her head. If she lived with a man, people would make rude assumptions about them. His presence in her life was going to bring about all sorts of gossip. Not only that, but surely he'd make the place stink like body odor or meat or something equally horrible, and he'd probably play music too loud and leave dishes in the sink. He might have a nice smile and warm eyes, but he still looked arrogant and obnoxious.

When she finally came out to the kitchen, she saw that he'd found the cabinets she'd left empty and was busy putting away what looked like a rather nice set of dishes.

"Can we talk about this like adults?" she asked.

"Sure." He didn't bother to look at her.

"What just happened in the hallway is exactly why we can't live together."

He turned to her with that self-confident smile. "I've seen girls in towels before."

She was sure he had. He knew he was good-looking—like Thor, only thinner, with short military-cut hair. Which was even more reason why they couldn't live together. "I had this all planned out," she said. "Everything was lined up. You are supposed to be a girl, not some creepy guy who just got an eyeful."

"What makes you think I'm creepy? I had nothing to do with you being in a towel."

"Because of the way you looked at me!"

He shook his head, but his voice was as calm as ever, even a little amused. "I was trying to introduce myself to my new roommate, who had just stepped into the hallway. I didn't know what you were wearing until I'd already said your name."

"Did you state on the application that you're a girl?" She jutted out a hip. "Were you trying to connive your way into a female roommate?"

"Connive?" He pulled his phone from the back pocket of his jeans. "I'll show you my application."

Allie waited impatiently, looking anywhere but at him. Something in their marshy backyard caught her eye. "Oh my God," she whispered, as if the beast might hear her. "I think there's a wolf out there."

"Naw, that's Buttercup."

"That is not little Buttercup." The long-legged raggedy-looking gray mongrel could easily eat small dogs for breakfast.

"I never said Cuppie was little." He stepped next to her to show her the rental application on his phone, and she realized how very tall he was. She didn't want to feel small and feminine next to him. She wanted to feel mad. "Right here," he said, noting the checkmark next to the word *male*. "But I did say that I had no preference on my roommate's gender."

"Then the rental company messed up," Allie said. "Because I specifically said female." Now that he was so near, she distinctly smelled soap, her favorite scent. And his eyes had smile lines beside them, which only served to make her dislike him more. She leaned away from him. "I can't deal with this. I start my dream job tomorrow and I need to be well-rested and"—she didn't know how to finish the sentence—"man-free."

He nodded like he was appraising her. "Got it. I'm steel, you're silk. I'll do my best to keep my high testosterone ways from bothering you." He tucked his phone into his back pocket and went back to putting dishes and coffee mugs in his cabinet.

Silk? She didn't know if she should be flattered or offended. But she did know that her morning was ruined and her entire year might be too. She had to get out of this house, away from Sam Clare. Even though she'd just taken a shower, she needed a run. She would have to go longer than usual in order to deal with the surprise of her awful new roommate. She had at least seven miles' worth of frustration in her.

Running was the one constant in Allie's life. It had been ever since joining the cross-country team in junior high. She changed quickly and hit the ground at a warm-up pace, already feeling better. She'd only been on Goose Island two weeks, but she was already getting used to the swampy terrain and the briny smell of pluff mud, which on warmer days reeked of rotten eggs.

According to her running app, she was two miles in. The sidewalk had long since started cracking and rising up with roots as she ran in the shade of old oaks and palmettos and overgrown greenery that occasionally opened to ponds marked by alligator warning signs. Her breathing was steady and her feet sure. Parked outside her neighbor's old low-slung brick house was a bright yellow food truck with the words SALTY DOT'S painted in blue curlicues on the side. Each time she saw it, she was reminded to track it down and try the food. Aside from the sandwiches and barbecue made by an old guy named Fred at the local gas station, there were no other restaurants on Goose Island.

If she didn't have to hit her nine-minute-mile goal, she would slow down to look closer at the windows of Salty Dot's old home, where it seemed like a different color cat sat on the sill of every front window. She covered her cold nose with her hand, wishing she'd worn her neck gaiter so she could pull it up for warmth. Back in Nashville, a gaiter was a running necessity on cold and snowy days. She didn't even know if South Carolina got snow. But it didn't matter. Snow was for cozy nights and white Christmases, and she was actively trying to minimize Christmas—not ignore, not skip, just scrape through unscathed.

Allie took care to avoid stepping on the sidewalk cracks and lines, but most importantly, at the end of the run she must land with her right foot on the front porch welcome mat. If she didn't, disaster would follow—someone would get hurt or something in her life would go wrong. She had learned to tell from a fairly long distance which foot she would end on, and lengthened her stride to make sure.

The chill of the wind in her face and the steady cadence of her breathing was helping. Sam Clare wasn't going to ruin things for her. She simply wouldn't allow it. Every successful roommate scenario included rules and boundaries. Simple.

She'd come to her favorite part of the run—the stage where she felt like she could go on forever. But she was now back on Evergreen Way, past Salty Dot's for the second time, and her app was nearing exactly seven miles. Seven because it symbolized a connection between the mortal realm and higher places. Spiritual places, like where her dad was—somewhere in heaven.

The quaint white clapboard cottage came into sight. She'd loved it since the first time she saw it online. It had two bedrooms, one bathroom, and a nice large kitchen that opened up onto a family room and a screened-in back porch. The furniture she'd had in her Nashville apartment fit perfectly in the space. Her creamy rugs toned down the dark oak floors, and her antique landscape paintings brought the green from outside in. Her things combined with the existing dainty yellow-flowered wallpaper and chipping white metal chandelier felt perfectly cozy until Sam showed up. The dude probably came with a lava lamp, or worse, a gaming system.

She landed with her right foot on the front porch mat, and that eased her mind, but she still wasn't ready to go inside. She made her way around the outside of the house and across the backyard to the dock on the salt marsh. It was a little chilly outside, but her body would stay warm from the run for a while. She sat at the very end on the cold, splintery wood and looked beyond the marsh hay to the water, watching pelicans fly overhead and listening to the *pop-pop-pop* of clams buried in the muddy shore.

Carefully, she scooted her sitz bones so that she wasn't touching the crack between wood slats, then did the same with her heels, hugging her knees. Her stomach grumbled. There was no way to avoid it: she was going to have to face her new roommate. She set the timer on her watch for exactly three minutes, then tested herself to see if she could be like one of Pavlov's conditioned rats and know exactly when the bell would ring.

She did.

"I need to eat breakfast," she said when she found Sam still in the kitchen putting cans of food in the pantry. She'd already reconciled that he hadn't meant to surprise her, but she couldn't pretend that she was comfortable with her new living situation.

"Yeah," he said. "There's fried chicken in—"

"I know," she interrupted. Who ate fried chicken for breakfast? "That's yours. We might as well set up boundaries now."

"So I can stay?" He pretended to be pleasantly surprised.

"I didn't say that." She rifled through the refrigerator and pulled out a tub of cottage cheese and a bowl of washed blueberries. "You can have the top shelf of the refrigerator since you're taller. And the left side of the freezer."

"Yes, ma'am, boss lady."

She flinched. She'd been called bossy before. Well, her

whole life, really. "It's probably better if you don't speak to me right now."

He saluted her and went back to work.

She sat at the table eating her meal, trying not to be obvious about watching him from the corner of her eye. "Please tell me your dog isn't aggressive."

"Am I allowed to talk now?" He chuckled. "Cuppie's well-trained. She won't bother you unless I let her."

Allie regarded the huge dog staring at her through the glass door leading to the back porch. She took another bite of cottage cheese, then got up to retrieve a bottle of PH water from the refrigerator. "Good. She stays out of my room and off the couch."

"Yes, ma'am. Any more rules I need to know about?"

Truthfully, there were probably 2,352 more rules, but she would introduce him to those slowly. "I need quiet after ten P.M. but would prefer earlier, if possible."

"Cool." He seemed to find her amusing, which was highly annoying. "I'll tell all of my party chicks to keep it down."

She choked on her spoonful of cottage cheese and was grateful she had water nearby. *Chicks?* As in *women*? Even if he was kidding, it was totally uncalled for.

Living with Sam Clare was going to be horrible. Absolutely dreadful.

Chapter Two

"CHEROPHOBIA, SWEETHEART. I believe that's what it's called."

"Mama," Allie said. "Do not say words like that to me. I am not afraid to be happy, and I know that happiness does not cause things to go wrong. Please, stop trying to diagnose me." Great. Now she was going to have the word *cherophobia* running through her brain for God only knew how long.

"Well, you need to think more positively and start going out and doing fun things."

Allie heard loud snoring in the background, and she knew exactly who it was. Her mother's boyfriend was sleeping over. A burning sensation exploded in her stomach, and she didn't try to hold back her venom. "Like you did? I just need to go to a bar and latch on to the first man who looks my way? That's gonna bring me happiness?" It was barely six A.M. and she was already fighting with her mother.

"Allie, darling, that is not at all what I said. And not what I did either."

"I have to get to work. This conversation is not helping to put me in the right frame of mind for my first day."

"Okay, then. Well, I just wanted to call and wish you good luck."

Allie exhaled her exasperation loud enough for her mother to hear. "Bye, Mama."

"Bye, sweetheart."

She was sick of cheerful, fake, smiling robot-people who pretended like life was great all the time. Given a choice, she'd rather be unhappy. Anyway, she was in the middle of adapting to a new place, a new roommate, and a new job. Adaptation took time. As a matter of fact, when she looked it up online, it said to plan for an entire year to make the transition. Not only was she completely alone, but now she had to tolerate things like the muddy size-twelve shoes left by the front door, dog hair all over the floor, and the freaking stocking hung on the fireplace mantel—a cheap red one that looked like it came from the Dollar Store. Sam had better be going somewhere else for Christmas, because she would not be spending it at home with him.

Allie opened her bedroom blinds to find the early fog burning off. Dainty yellow streams of sun entered the room and illuminated the floating dust motes like glitter. She turned on the soothing twang of country music and immediately felt worse. The sweet simplicity of the music cut through the self-serving chaos of life to an uncomplicated core of love and family. It was that core she missed—knowing she had something stable, something permanent. Any stability she once had was gone forever. She stared at the twinkling dust and wished their soft airlessness could bring her happiness, but it was too soon for that. There were supposed to be stages of grief, and she was firmly in the anger phase.

Allie stuffed her feet into a new pair of black heels and made sure her white silk shirt was tucked perfectly into her trousers. The streaming sun made her hair glow an especially brilliant dark red, and she chose to wear it in a low bun so that she wouldn't attract as much attention as when it hung free and long. *Duke Bradley*, she thought, double-checking with herself that she got the name right. He was the old man who owned the Saltwater Winery, and the one who'd chosen her for her first-ever job using her bachelor's degree in food science and her master's in enology.

At first she wasn't sure that the Saltwater Winery's muscadine wine could taste good—usually it was as sweet as sugar syrup, but after trying them all, several of the wines were dry and good enough even for her picky palate. As an enologist, she would make sure the grapes were harvested with the right sugar and acid levels to make the best vintages. She was excited to analyze the wines and help make them as good as they could be. Growing up with a father who loved fine wines had its advantages. She saw her choice of career, and her new job, as somewhat of an ode to him.

Thankfully, Sam was not in the kitchen when she made herself a to-go cup of coffee for the ten-minute drive to the tip of the island. She was free to think and not have to make small talk. She grabbed a protein bar from her private cupboard and wobbled and *click-clicked* in her uncomfortable shoes toward the foyer. It was okay that she'd missed that year's grape harvest, because it would give her time to put her skills to use slowly instead of jumping into chaos. She locked the front door and balanced her way down the concrete steps toward her car. Mr. Bradley said there was one other enologist she would be working with, a man named Joey Amato. She remembered the name because it sounded Italian—did he come from a long line of winemakers? He was supposed to meet her this morning to help get her started.

She had one leg inside her car when a loud bark lurched her sideways and straight into the car's metal frame. She screamed as the wolf snarled and bared its teeth like she was a carjacker about to receive the jaws of justice.

"Buttercup!" Sam's deep voice called out. "Come!"

The dog immediately left Allie and ran to Sam's side.

"Heel," he said, and the dog fell into step beside him, looking more like a wolf with her extra-long canine teeth bared and shocking bright yellow eyes.

Allie held on to the doorframe and tried to catch her breath. Her head pounded only slightly slower than her heart.

"Cuppie shouldn't have done that," Sam said when he got closer. "She's been out of service too long, I guess."

Allie slunk into the front seat, holding her head.

"Are you hurt?" he asked.

She shot him her best leave-me-alone look. Wasn't he the one who claimed to have complete control over the dog? He'd probably ordered her to attack. "I have to get to work."

"Stay," he said to Buttercup, and for a second, Allie thought he was talking to her. Without permission, he kneeled in front of her and gently moved her hand from her forehead. He was so tall that, even while kneeling, he was the same height as her in the driver's seat. "It didn't break the skin, but it's already bruising. I'll get you some ice."

"I don't have time for ice," she said, mad that her eyes were hot with tears. She blinked them away. "I won't be late on my first day." Didn't he know that her job was everything? It was the sole reason she was on an overgrown tiny island with more wildlife than people, and it was the only thing she cared about anymore. Turning from him, she buckled her seat belt, thereby indicating that he needed to move so she could shut the door.

He stood and stepped aside.

Damn dog. Damn roommate. Her breath was shallow and tight. She needed to compartmentalize the experience immediately—tuck it away and tie it up in the part of her brain where it would quietly simmer until it, hopefully, evaporated completely. When Sam acted like he cared, it was too much like having her dad back. It made her feel vulnerable, and she couldn't tolerate that. Her car kicked up dust from the long pea gravel driveway and she hoped it sent Sam into a coughing fit. His dog too. He hadn't even apologized. There was no way she was going to live with a guy like that for an entire year, and she wasn't going to be the one to leave. The little cottage was too perfect—the location near work, the backyard that led to the marsh, the back porch with the haint-blue ceiling, the little dock set up for crabbing and fishing, and the rope swing hanging from one of the many old oaks dotting the property. Not to mention how perfectly her antique four-poster bed fit in her room, with plenty of space for the padded bench at the bottom, the highboy dresser she'd thrifted and painted white, and her dad's old easy chair in the corner. No, Sam would be the one to leave.

The ten-minute drive to work felt like an hour. Between the word *cherophobia* chomping around in her brain like Pac-Man and the bruise on her head starting to swell, she felt all sorts of discombobulated. Plus, the coffee was making her jittery. By the time she reached the sprawling fifty acres of the Saltwater Winery, she was only five minutes early, when she'd planned for twenty. Five minutes was just long enough to walk from the gravel parking lot past the lines of dormant trellised grapevines to the long tin-roofed building that housed the gift shop and the business office portion of the winery. There was no time to decompress, and no time to go home and change shoes—the gravel was already scratching the leather and ruining the heel tips.

"Good." Duke Bradley stood unsmiling inside the wide-open front door, waving her inside. "We've been waiting for you."

She panicked and checked her watch. She still had two minutes left. "Am I late?"

"You should've worn comfortable shoes."

She could've told him that. "I'll do that tomorrow."

"We're farmers," he said as he led her into the building. "We don't dress up."

"Yes, sir." She'd known he was a grumpy old man when she took the job, but this was not the warm welcome she was hoping for. He led her through the gift shop, which was decorated for Christmas and filled with as many wine-related gifts as gorgeous home accents. There was even an entire wall dedicated to local painters and potters, along with fresh poinsettias from an island greenhouse. How could a man this grouchy curate such beautiful things?

They passed through a back door behind the register into a hallway lined with offices, and stopped at a door with a nameplate that read JOEY AMATO, ENOLOGIST. "We'll add your name," Duke said. "You share this office with Joey."

"Thank you." She stepped inside the small square room outfitted with two back-to-back desks along opposite walls, two computers, a large bookshelf, and a filing cabinet. It was like an oversized closet with a sliding glass door on the back wall that led into a small white laboratory. A man sat with his feet up on one of the desks. From behind, he looked way too familiar. The straight across cut of his short dark hair, the broad shoulders... If she didn't already know his name was Joey, she'd think he was her ex-boyfriend, Mark.

Just one year ago, Mark up and moved to California in the middle of their happy relationship, thereby completely shattering her heart. He'd blamed the breakup on job opportunities and timing, and she'd never forgiven him. What kind of man could claim to love a person and then toss her back into her miserable single life like catch-and-release? As she held her breath, Joey Amato slow-motion set his feet down and swiveled his chair to face her.

He looked just enough like Mark to make her face go hot and her stomach lurch.

In the amount of time it took for Joey to stand and extend his hand, Allie had already reprimanded herself twelve different ways for imagining the possibility that she might have a relationship with her coworker. Her brain was as rogue as ocean waves after a hurricane.

"Hi, I'm Allie. Nice to meet you." His hand was soft and warm, like a man who spent most of his days at a computer or a microscope. She smiled sweetly at him as her mind continued its argument—*You do not need a man. He is not Mark. It isn't fair to substitute Joey for Mark. It is your loneliness speaking. This won't solve anything. And anyway, his nose is too big.*

Joey looked at the knot on her forehead, which she quickly covered with the hand that just shook his. "I had a little mishap with a wolf and my car this morning," she chuckled, trying to make light of it.

"You hit a wolf? I didn't know we had any on the island."

Why did she say wolf? It was overly dramatic. "My roommate's dog looks like a wolf. It scared me as I was getting into the car." Great. Now he thought she was an embellisher. "No big deal. I'm fine."

"Goose Island has coyotes," Duke interjected disapprovingly, "not wolves."

Allie had forgotten that Duke was still standing behind her. Just as she initiated a fantasy about yanking off her heels and sprinting back to her car, a sweet singsongy Southern voice rang down the hallway. "I brought gingerbread cookies! Y'all should come get some while they're still warm."

Duke pivoted without a word, grabbed a cookie from the beautiful blonde in the hallway, and shuffled away.

"Oh, hey!" the girl said. "You must be Allison. I'm Jessa Boone. We're all so glad to have you part of the Saltwater family."

"Thank you. You can call me Allie." Her mother was the only person who still called her Allison.

"Take some cookies. Mama made them fresh this morning. Oh, and the truck'll be outside for lunch. Hope y'all didn't pack your own."

"Salty Dot's?" Allie asked, suddenly hopeful that the day might improve even though she'd brought a container of lentil soup from home.

"Yes!" Jessa said like a happy little cheerleader. "Today she's got shrimp po'boys and pimiento cheeseburgers."

"I think your mama might be my neighbor," Allie said with the most enthusiasm she'd felt all day.

Jessa squinted at her. "Oh my word! You're the girl who's been jogging past our house!"

Allie nodded. So, they'd seen her. "I keep wanting to stop and see the cats."

"Little monsters," she said. "Knock next time! And go say hi to Mama today. The truck'll pull in around eleven. I just know she's gonna want to meet you." She held the plate out to Joey, who took a cookie. Then she offered it to Allie. Allie didn't like gingerbread, but it would be rude to say no. As soon as she had the cookie in her hand, Jessa turned and yelled, "Libby!"

"What?" came a female voice from the next office.

"Gingerbread!"

"Can't do it," the voice, which must belong to a person named Libby, said. "You know my wedding's coming up."

"Just a sec," Jessa said, leaving to pop her head into an open door one office down. "You can't be on a diet at Christmas, Libs. Just take a cookie."

"I don't like gingerbread," Libby said.

"You'll like these."

"Stop trying to make me too big for my dress."

"Just eat one." Jessa held a cookie out to her.

"Enough with the peer pressure already." Libby's voice

rose, and it did not sound amused.

"I'll just leave one on your desk."

"If you step one foot into my office, I will punch you in the head."

"Starving girls are so touchy," Jessa laughed.

"Get away from me before I call the sheriff."

Jessa's cheerful disposition never wavered. "Aw, how sweet of you. More people to try my mama's cookies." She practically skipped down the hall to the next office.

Allie turned back to her new office and her new office mate.

"Welcome to the winery of the weird and wacky," Joey said. "I promise you won't be bored."

And with that, Allie set down her bags, pulled up her new black swivel chair, and turned her back on Joey Amato.

Chapter Three

OF COURSE ALLIE worked overtime on her first day at work—she knew how to make a good first impression. As a matter of fact, there was so much to familiarize herself with that she worked through lunch too. She would have to meet Salty Dot another time. When she finally pulled in front of her little white cottage, she was so hungry she almost didn't notice that it was glowing like a lantern in the darkness. Someone, namely Sam, had added little white twinkle lights to the front eaves, and turned on the porch lights. After an exhausting day, it felt like the house was welcoming her home.

She looked around for the dog before stepping out of the car and nearly twisted an ankle when her phone dinged. It was a text from Joey.

"Stopping by Fred's before work tomorrow. What's your coffee order?"

Joey wanted to buy her a coffee? Did that mean he liked her? He'd been nice but kind of quiet all day. Her heart skipped a beat.

"I would love that! Thank you so much. I don't know the

choices, but a double espresso with oat milk and one Splenda would be great."

As soon as she sent it, she regretted it. This wasn't Nashville, and she'd just made herself appear high maintenance. Did Fred's gas station even offer anything aside from plain black with powdered creamer? It was going to take some time to get used to living on an island with only one old dilapidated building to get gas, toilet paper, or a turkey sandwich. The place looked like it was holding on to the 1940s with its old SUNBEAM BREAD signs and chipping, hand-painted graphics that promised GAS, OIL, and LUNCH on the side of the concrete building. She texted again.

"Just a plain black coffee is great too. Anything works. Thank you again."

The exhaustion she'd been feeling was replaced by giddiness. Instead of dragging herself inside, she practically skipped barefoot up the cold stairs, holding her painful, ruined heels in one hand and opening the door with the other. It had to mean something good that Joey was bringing her coffee tomorrow.

The first thing she saw when she made it past the landing was a Christmas tree in the den. It was complete with colorful lights, ornaments, and a big gold star on top. She dropped her shoes onto the wooden floor with two thuds. Sam hadn't even discussed it with her. What if she was allergic to pine? What if she was of a religion that didn't celebrate Christmas? Her plan was firmly to sit alone on a beach and eat her dad's favorite ham and pickle sandwich.

That purposefully did not include the traditional things that her mother always insisted on, like decorated trees. He'd just brought one into her home without asking.

She backed up against the door as she noticed the wolf-dog staring at her. "Get your dog!" she yelled, louder than necessary.

"Cuppie, come!" Sam's deep voice bellowed from the kitchen. Buttercup instantly turned and ran to him. That's when Allie realized the house smelled good. Like food. He better not have made a mess of the stovetop. And he'd better move aside because she needed to make herself dinner too. "You hungry?" he asked as she turned the corner. "I've got plenty."

He was slicing thick chunks of pot roast out of a Crock-Pot and adding it to his plate of carrots and mashed potatoes. Her mother used to make the same meal for them at least once a month. It was like Susie Westley was somehow manipulating the world to make her daughter think of her. Allie hadn't answered yet, and Sam was already getting one of his plates from the cupboard for her.

"Thanks," she said, giving in to the smell. She took a seat on a counter barstool.

He filled her plate and put it in front of her before walking around the island to sit beside her with Cuppie at his feet. "How was your day?" he asked.

She gave him the side-eye.

"Your head feeling okay?"

The swelling had gone down, and she was left with a dime-sized purplish bruise above her eyebrow. "It's fine."

They ate in silence for a while. "This is good," she finally said.

"It took me some time to cook again after getting hit. My left arm still doesn't work well, but it does enough."

"Hit by what?"

"A five-five-six."

"What's a five-five-six?"

"A NATO round. The standard used by the military."

"A bullet?"

He nodded.

"You were shot?"

He pointed at the biceps on his left arm, then took a bite of food like they weren't talking about what had to be an extremely traumatic experience for him.

"Was it an accident?"

"Naw." He chewed and swallowed. "Armed conflict."

"Like, war? Are you in the army?"

He chuckled. "I was. So was Cup. But we're not anymore."

"What do you do now?"

"A bunch of stuff. Consulting mostly. But I also work as a paramedic in Charleston, and Cup and I volunteer with the local rescue squad."

It sounded like he could pay his rent, so that was good.

"Cup and I are building a house on the island too."

Good, she thought, pushing aside feelings of admiration. He wasn't planning to live in the cottage forever. "When will it be ready?"

"It's gonna take at least a year."

Well, that was a disappointment. The dog lay down, and she flinched. Every time Cuppie moved, Allie got a shot of adrenaline.

"She won't hurt you," he said. "I promise."

"Right," she said beneath her breath. Tell that to her bruised forehead. She took another bite. God, the pot roast was good. Better than her mama's. "I feel like I need to warn you: I am doing Christmas differently this year. I don't want all the hype. So, if you're planning to have a party or something like that, I'd appreciate some advance notice."

He acknowledged her statement by looking straight at her with piercing hazel eyes. He must've decided not to pry because he turned and went back to eating.

"I mean, the tree and the lights and all?" She gestured toward the tree by the fireplace. "They're fine. But I need to focus on this job, and my daddy's gone now, and I'm not going to spend the holiday with Mama and her boyfriend, so I'm celebrating in my own way. Alone."

He nodded but said nothing.

"I mean, I'm not sad about it or anything."

He nodded again, and that time she found his silence infuriating. It felt like that morning when he didn't apologize for his dog. She was beginning to figure him out—if he didn't agree with something or didn't want to do something, he did nothing. She stood to take her plate to the sink.

"Are you trying to punish yourself for something?" he blurted.

Allie froze. What kind of an intrusive question was that? "Of course not. And it's extremely rude for you to ask." She scraped the food scraps into the sink disposal a little too aggressively.

"Christmas traditions might be good for you. There's a reason why they've been passed down for generations."

"You sound like my mother."

"Just asking," he said, shrugging only with his right shoulder. He'd piled so much food on his plate that he still had a lot to eat.

She put her dishes in the dishwasher and wiped her hands on her dish towel before heading to her room, even though what she really wanted to do was sit on the couch and watch a mindless reality show. It wasn't even seven o'clock yet.

"How long ago did your dad die?" Sam asked before she got away.

She paused. "Almost three years."

"He died at Christmastime?"

Just the acknowledgment made her stomach burn and pressure fill her head. "Three days before."

"So, the last couple of Christmases have been hard for you."

"Right."

He seemed pleased with himself.

"I mean, I'm fine. It's just that with my dad gone, my mother insists on overdoing everything. I want a Christmas that doesn't revolve around her for once."

The way he looked at her so intently made her want to cover his eyes with both hands.

"Mama has a boyfriend now, okay? I'm not being mean. She just doesn't need me."

He stayed silent, like he was waiting for her to say more.

"Now that you got what you wanted, am I good to leave?" She noted that she sounded sassy and felt a pang of guilt.

"There's a new episode of *Single and Searching* dropping tonight," he said.

It was almost like he knew her. Or maybe he just thought she was shallow. Or desperate. She didn't have time to answer before the doorbell rang. "One of your chicks?" She smirked.

Even though she was already up and he hadn't yet finished his dinner, he stood to get the door. Cuppie went with him, and Allie let them pass, noting that his left arm wasn't as muscular as his right. For a guy like him, that had to be a difficult thing to deal with. He probably couldn't do push-ups or pull-ups or carry heavy things, and clearly, he was the kind of guy who prided himself on that sort of thing.

"Well, hey there, y'all!" It was Jessa in all of her perfect blonde Barbie-esque glory. "This is my mama, Dottie, and my little sister, Tulip." She stepped aside so they could get a good look at the middle-aged woman wearing a royal-blue knit beanie and the lanky middle-schooler with the bowl haircut. When the older woman smiled, she was missing a bottom tooth. "Sorry for barging in, but we wanted to bring y'all a welcome gift."

Dottie handed them a paper bag. "In these parts, a neighbor is already a friend, and since we're a cookin' family, we thought y'all might appreciate some of our famous tuna salad. The trick is to add a touch of Worcestershire sauce before you add the mayonnaise."

"Come in," Sam said. "I'm Sam, and this is Buttercup." Cuppie sat on her haunches, perfectly docile, but still looking like a badass wolf.

"Don't be letting that dog out around my cats, ya hear? They like to wander." Dottie wasn't budging from the front porch.

"Cuppie won't bother your cats," he promised.

"And keep him out of the marsh or a gator'll get him like they did my Rudy."

Jessa piped in, "Rudy was a fat orange cat."

"We ain't stayin'," Dottie said. "Just wanted to properly introduce ourselves. I woulda brought y'all more fish salad if I'd known there was a man over here."

Allie was relieved they were leaving. She suddenly felt possessive of Sam, like she had dibs on him. If Jessa was to stay, he'd be in love with her by the time she sat on the couch with a glass of sweet tea. Allie watched him say goodbye. It might already be too late.

What was happening to her? Could she not be around a good-looking man without wanting him for herself? She tapped her middle finger three times against her hip. Then again. And again. It'd been a year since Mark, one full year since she'd had any real affection from a man. Her body must be entering desperation mode.

She needed to shut that down immediately.

Chapter Four

SOMEWHERE AROUND TWO in the morning, Sam started screaming. Like, literally yelling out commands while still asleep. *Former army*, she remembered. Five-five-six. NATO bullets. She lay there listening, wondering whether she should do something. But if she was honest, she was also afraid. When she heard furniture crashing, she threw on her bathrobe and ran into his room. It took a minute to find the light switch, and when she did, he was crouched behind his overturned dresser, white T-shirts and black underwear spilling out from the drawers.

"I can't find my weapon!" he screamed at her, frantic. "Where's my weapon?!"

"Sam!" She was afraid to approach him. "Sam! Wake up!"

"Get down! Left! It's coming from the left!"

"Sam!"

Buttercup barked from inside the closet. Allie quickly opened the door. "Buttercup! What are you doing in there?"

The dog ran over to Sam and nudged him with her nose before squeezing her entire body between him and the dresser. Sam decompressed, slouched, petted Cuppie, and woke up. The first thing he noticed when he came to was Allie standing in the doorway.

He rubbed his hand back and forth over his short hair, his face red and sweaty. "How much did you see?"

"Are you okay?" She needed to know. She was scared to death for him.

"This doesn't happen often. I promise."

She squatted near him and asked again. "Are you okay?"

"Not always."

"What do you need? What can I do for you?"

"Water would be great."

Even though he'd just experienced something far different than her occasional panic attacks, whenever she had an episode, she needed ice-cold water afterward too. She filled a glass with ice before adding water from her filtration pitcher in the refrigerator. When she came back in, the dresser had been righted, the clothes cleaned up, and Sam was sitting on the edge of his bed in his underwear. She immediately noticed his scarred left arm, but not before his abs gave her a jolt of something she hadn't felt for a long time. Her hand shook as she gave him the glass.

"Thanks," he said. "You should go back to bed. You have work in the morning."

"I won't leave until I know you've recovered."

"I'm fine."

The dog lay on the bed beside him, but her eyes were

wide open and a little wild. "Is Cuppie okay? She was locked in the closet."

"Yeah, I do that. When I get these night terrors, I always try to protect her."

Protect her from what? From himself?

FRED MADE SURPRISINGLY good coffee. There was no oat milk, but fresh cream from a nearby dairy worked just fine. Allie took a sip and tried to focus on the computer screen. She was at work, back-to-back with Joey at the desk behind her. She would look up night terrors on her lunch break. There should be plenty of time since Dottie's food truck wasn't here today. Thank goodness for the tuna salad currently stashed in her insulated lunch bag.

"Fred started smoking brisket last night," Joey said, spinning around. "It smelled so good this morning, I can't stop thinking about it."

She turned her chair around to face him. "You know, I was actually afraid of Fred's place when I first saw it. It's kind of like a Nashville speakeasy—not at all what it looks like on the outside." To look at it was to think it'd been closed and left to decay for decades.

"This is my favorite time of year at the station. Fred dresses up like Santa. Grows out his beard and all. If we don't get that brisket soon, it'll be gone by noon. Let's take an early lunch." He said it like it was a foregone conclusion that they would be having lunch together.

Given the cold freezer pack she put in with the tuna salad, it should survive until tomorrow. "Sounds good. I love brisket."

"Cool," he said, spinning his chair back to face his desk. "We'll leave at eleven."

She stared at her computer screen, stuck in her thoughts. What would people think if she and Joey went out to lunch together? Were there rules against dating your coworker? She didn't want to risk her job, no matter how much Joey looked like Mark with a bigger nose. "Should we invite Jessa or Libby?"

"We can if you want to." He didn't sound very enthusiastic. They both spun their chairs around at the same time. "I mean, Jessa will probably be there anyway," he said. "Fred's her uncle, so when her mother isn't running the food truck, that's where she goes."

It was beginning to feel like everyone on the island was related. "Should we invite Libby so she won't feel left out?"

"Naw, she won't go. She's on some sort of bird diet where she only eats seeds and nuts."

"Seriously?"

"I don't actually know what kind of diet it is. But she said she will off anyone who eats in front of her. If she smelled that brisket, she'd probably kill us all."

Allie had only met Libby once. She was the sole employee in the Saltwater Winery's marketing department, and it was probably good that she didn't have to answer to anyone aside from Duke. Despite her fancy monogrammed purse and pearl necklace, the woman seemed fully capable of, and maybe even predisposed toward, murder. "Okay, skip her," Allie said. There were tons of other employees, but most of them worked in the field, in the tasting room, cellar, gift shop, or bottling plant, and she hadn't met them yet.

So, it looked like she had a date with Joey. Alone.

"Come get me in the lab when you're ready," she said.

The truth was, she needed to get away from the computer. She hadn't gone for a run in two days. Every time she tried to type out a report, she would compulsively hit the delete button. It took her twice as long as it should to get it done. And the lack of sleep wasn't helping. She desperately needed exercise and a nap.

"Hey, Al?" Jessa popped her head into the sterile lab. "Your roomie's here to see you."

The glass pipette Allie held nearly slipped from her grip. "Sam's here?"

"Yup. And, as my mother would say, that man is hotter than the inside of my deep fryer."

"Shoot. I need to finish this. Can you tell him I'll be there in, like, ten minutes?" She checked her watch. It was nearing eleven o'clock. Why was Sam here? His timing was terrible. Now Joey was going to know that her roommate was a man and wonder about them. Wonder about *her*.

Actually, everyone at her place of employment was probably going to wonder what was going on between her self and Sam. *Dammit.* Her private life was supposed to be just that—private. She wanted to be seen as a highly educated professional enologist, not a single woman living with a random hot guy and going out to lunch with her attractive male coworker. She felt her face redden as she tried to come up with a plan for dealing with Sam. And Joey.

Ten minutes later, she still hadn't decided what to do as she stepped outside and saw Sam and Cuppie waiting for her by Duke's flower garden. Actually, it was Duke's dead wife's garden, as indicated by the sign over the arched arbor entryway that said AMELIA'S PATCH OF HAPPINESS. Duke was always in there planting and pruning and generally looking glum, and she prayed he wasn't there now to see his newest employee leaving her desk to talk with a man and his wolf-dog.

Sam brazenly kept his eyes on her as she walked toward them, which made her question if she was walking weird. She looked around at everything except him, grateful that she wasn't wearing heels.

"Hey," she said as she approached. "Everything okay?"

"I think we should exchange phone numbers," he said. "I couldn't text to make sure you're okay. Rough night last night."

"Here," she said, extending her hand. He placed his phone on her palm, and she entered her number. "You're right. We probably should have that information." The clock on his phone said 10:55.

"Yeah, and Cup's been a little off all morning, so I thought it might do her some good to see you and have an outing." He looked around at the huge oaks, wooden picnic tables, rope swings, cornhole games, and colorful metal wine bottle trees dotting the acreage all the way down to the water. It was like a rustic resort except that it didn't have a hotel. "Nice place to work."

"Good wines too." She bent down to pet Cuppie. It was the first time she'd ever shown the dog affection, and Cuppie seemed okay, if not flat-out happy, about it. She wagged her tail and made a sweet whining sound. Maybe the drama of the night before had created some sort of trauma bond between them. "Feel free to walk around," Allie said. "There's wine tasting inside if you like that kind of thing."

"I went into town for groceries this morning, and I can make us some lunch if you want to come back to the house. Do you get a lunch break?"

"An hour," she said. "But I'm sorry. I already made plans." Joey was probably looking for her at that very moment.

"Alright." Sam seemed completely unbothered by her refusal. "I'll have dinner ready when you get home."

"You don't need to make me dinner!" She may have said it a little too strenuously. What was a he? A house husband? He was being way too nice. "It's probably not smart to set up these sorts of expectations. You do you, and I'll do me. Okay?"

"It's just for now," he said. "Cup and I will be getting busy with the house soon, and I figure if I'm gonna cook for myself, I can cook for my roommate too. It's no big deal."

The way he said it seemed perfectly logical, and the pot roast he'd made had been the best meal she'd had in weeks. Months, maybe. She watched Duke putter around in the garden while she thought about it. "I don't know what time I'll be getting home. I'm new at this job, and I might need to work late. Thanks, though." Joey would be walking out any second, looking for her. "Sorry to be so short, but I need to get back to work."

"You don't have to eat dinner with me," he said. "I'll save you a plate." That was it. He'd made a definitive statement.

"Well, I can cook sometimes too." She wondered what the old man hunched over and sweating in the garden ate for dinner. Was he alone every night? Then she hoped that Sam liked chicken tenders and fruit. That was her go-to dinner.

When she turned away from Duke's garden, she was no longer standing with just Sam and Cuppie.

Joey was there too.

Chapter Five

To say there was an abundance of testosterone at Allie's lunch was an understatement. In her panic after Joey showed up, she lost control of her brain and her tongue and somehow managed to invite Sam to go with them. It was a nightmare—beginning with both men wanting her to ride in the car with them, Sam in his lifted Jeep, and Joey in his old black BMW. Allie denied both of them and drove herself, completely freaking out the entire way there. What was she going to talk to them both about? What if they hated each other? *Good Lord, good Lord, good Lord.* What had she gotten herself into? She checked her face in the rearview mirror to make sure her mascara wasn't smeared, then added a quick touch of lip gloss before she arrived.

Judging from the tiny parking lot, the whole island must have smelled the brisket. The one weathered picnic table out front had people sitting thigh-to-thigh. Other folks sat on the backs of their tailgates or walked out of the station with white paper to-go bags. Allie thought she recognized Dottie's voice yelling out names, and it was confirmed when she walked in and saw the signature blue beanie. Sam and Joey were already in line, and yes, they were talking to each other. What would be worse than those two as rivals? Those two as friends.

The tiny store bustled with chatter and loud orders of brisket with potato salad, macaroni salad, or fruit salad. Some people stopped just short of shoving each other, and others flashed fake smiles, but they all had an undercurrent of *I'm just here for the meat.* Behind the counter was a tall man with a white beard dressed all in red. The man was so deep into a different world that a sense of urgency did not exist for him. She couldn't hear it, but he was probably calmly humming "Silent Night" as he scooped mounds of salad beside the slices of smoked meat.

"Bubba Atkins!" Dottie yelled. "Your order's ready!"

A thick man with a mullet underneath his camo ball cap forced his way to the counter.

"Hold tight to that sauce cup," Dottie said. "Don't let it fall off the plate." Then she checked her phone and frowned before scanning the crowd for someone. Her eyes landed on Allie. "Hey, neighbor," she said. "You know where my Carolina Jessamine's at?"

Allie quickly thought back through her morning, noting each time she'd seen Jessa walk past her office. "I saw her earlier, but I don't know if she left the winery for lunch yet."

"If you see her, tell her to call her mother."

"Yes, ma'am," Allie said. "I sure will." She would absolutely track Jessa down as soon as she got back to work.

"Dewayne!" Dottie yelled toward the man Allie knew as Fred. "You heard from Tulip?"

Dewayne/Fred/Santa, whoever he was, stopped shoveling food onto plates and shook his head. "Not a peep."

"The school said she left after the second bell, and she ain't answerin' her phone. I can't get ahold of Carolina Jessamine neither."

"Well, I don't much like that," he said. "Why would she skip out?"

Dottie turned to Allie. "How much time you got?"

Allie glanced at her watch. "Like, forty-five minutes."

"Can you help my brother?" It was a desperate plea more than a question. "I've got to go."

"Of course." To be honest, it was a relief. Allie had just been given something to do that didn't involve awkward conversation with both her coworker and her roommate. She moved to the front of the line and squeezed behind the counter. Dottie gave her an apron and a rushed tutorial on how to use the old cash register before disappearing out the door.

Each time Fred handed her a tin-foil-covered paper plate, Allie would shout the name from the ticket he'd laid on top. "Scotty!" She handed the plate over the counter and past someone's head. "Davie! Mary Ellen!" In between yelling, she pecked at the old cash register that had probably been around since the 1980s. If someone wanted to use a credit card, Allie had to use Fred's personal cell phone. She actually found that part easier, having been her mother's assistant on several occasions when selling handmade candles at craft shows.

When it was Sam's turn to place his order, he offered to take over for her. The line was still practically out the door, and unless Dottie made it back soon, Allie was going to be taking an extra-long lunch break. Joey nodded like she should take him up on his offer. "Duke is a stickler about hours," he said. "Just put in your order with mine, and we'll take it back to the office."

It felt like a couple-y thing to say, but Joey was right. She needed to get back to work. "Thanks, Sam. Do you want me to drop Cuppie at home for you?"

Sam turned to Fred. "Okay for Cup to stay?"

"Put her out back. Whiskey'll watch her."

Sam opened the back door, and Allie got a glimpse of what she assumed was the place where Fred lived. It was a houseboat perched on top of cinder blocks and wood. There was a ladder to get up to it and lawn chairs set up around a firepit on the ground beside it. A huge brown dog ran up to them. His thick collar had a silver tag that said WHISKEY.

Fred's phone next to the cash register vibrated and rang. "Who is it?" he asked Allie with a knife in one hand and a thick slice of brisket in the other.

"It's Dottie."

"Answer it."

Dottie's voice was frantic. "I found Carolina Jessamine,

but Tulip's gone missing. Tell my brother that the jon boat's gone too. She done gone out on the water. She knows better—danged little brat. I tell you what, I'm gonna tan her behind when I find her."

Allie relayed the information to Fred. "The boat's gone. Dottie thinks Tulip took it out on the water."

Fred put down the scoop of macaroni salad and loudly yelled toward the crowd. "That's it. We're closing! Everybody out! If you already paid, I'll finish up those orders, but the rest of you need to git. We've got a family emergency."

He had another two huge smoked briskets and several tubs of side salads, but he was going to give it all up for his niece. Allie turned to Joey, who had his ear to his cell phone. He held up a finger, asking her to give him a second.

"Cuppie and I'll find her," Sam spoke up. "She's trained in search-and-rescue."

"Duke's cool with us taking the afternoon off," Joey said, hanging up. "We can stay and help Fred. Duke said he's gonna join the search too."

Fred, who was previously very much on a slow Southern schedule, had turned into a superfast serving machine. Joey made his way behind the counter and informed him that the customers didn't need to leave—he was taking over. Fred corrected his previous announcement with emotion in his voice and quickly disappeared the way Dottie had gone several minutes earlier.

"Cash only!" Fred yelled to the crowd as he popped back

in to retrieve his phone.

For the next hour, Allie and Joey worked side by side. It was fun, actually, and a great way to meet new people. The crowds died down just as the last few pieces of brisket were plated. Allie and Joey had never gotten any, so they made themselves a plate of side salads and picked at the remaining scraps of meat in the metal trays. They sat side by side on the counter to eat them. By then, her feet were pounding and her stomach was empty and complaining.

"This is not at all how I thought this day would go when I woke up this morning." She laughed.

"I told you Goose Island is weird and wacky."

"Do you think Tulip is okay?"

His face fell. "What is she, fourteen? Out on the ocean in a jon boat? I mean, she's a native. It's not her first time. She's probably fine." He looked at his phone, which had been set aside during the rush. "Jessa texted. She said thanks for helping out at the station. She and Duke are out on his boat searching."

Allie checked her phone too. There was nothing. "I'll text Sam."

A few seconds later, she got a response. *"We're at an abandoned camp across the waterway. We found her boat."*

Allie and Joey went to work setting up a group text to keep everybody in communication. In an instant, there was text after text of people saying they were on their way to the old Camp Dogwood. "I think we should go too," Allie said.

"Yeah." Joey jumped off the counter. "Let's lock up." They were able to lock the front door but left the back door unlocked with Whiskey at guard.

In his car, as a team, it felt right. Right to be with a smart man who had a good job. Right to be working together to help someone else. Right to be on a tiny island on the South Carolina coast, far away from Nashville. She touched the tip of her shoe to each of the four corners of the black floor mat and triple-checked that her seat belt was buckled. Now, if Tulip was just found safe and alive, Allie might actually be making progress toward being happy. Cherophobia could darn well stuff its *fear of happiness* crap into a rocket and shoot it to the moon.

Chapter Six

IT TOOK FORTY-FIVE minutes to drive to the overgrown green island that had just one narrow asphalt road, a camp, and a lighthouse. When they pulled into an old gravel parking lot and got out, they immediately heard voices calling out in beats like a metronome. "Tulip!" Silence. "Tulip!" Silence. "Tulip!"

So, they hadn't found her yet.

Allie and Joey walked past an old camp building down the slope to the water and found Dottie sitting in a jon boat flanked by one small and one large fishing boat. She knew from the group text that Sam had come over on the boat with Dottie and Fred. Probably the smaller one, considering the large boat was called the *Saltwater Duke*. "Dottie?" Allie called out. "You okay?"

She looked up and nodded, her blue beanie slumping down over her brow. "I'm focusing," she said. "Feeling her vibration. She's near water, but it's not the ocean." Dottie spread her arms across the width of the boat and lifted her head to the sun. Even though Allie had many questions, she kept quiet so the woman could concentrate. Dottie then stood so suddenly, the boat lurched and rocked. "Dammit," she said. "She's in the creek." She sat back down before she fell into the water and typed madly into her phone. Allie and Joey's phones dinged at the same time.

"She's in the creek somewhere. Dang girl is obsessed with finding shark teeth. She came out here looking. I know it."

From the top of the hill where an old brown building stood, sunny-haired Jessa came running. "Thank y'all so much for being here!" she said, somewhat out of breath. "Mama's right. Last year, Tulip knit 478 beanies and now she's moved on to shark teeth. Tootie's had it in her mind to find a megalodon tooth for months now. Probably heard she could find one out here and couldn't wait."

"The school said her cell phone's in a box in the science teacher's class," Dottie said. "Now we know we can't track her, so we better spread out wide."

"Come on, y'all," Jessa said, leading the way. "The creek's out this way. I used to come to this camp every summer, so I know this place better than a pirate making a treasure map."

"Like the back of a plan," Dottie said.

"Hand, mother," Jessa corrected. "I know it like the back of my hand." She pointed to a path leading into the woods. "Pass under the bridge and keep walking till you see the lighthouse, then head away from the beach. When y'all see the white birch tree, you're getting close." She jogged a few feet away before stopping again. "I'm gonna check the beach in case Mama's wrong about the creek. Her visions can get close to the truth, but they hardly ever land right on it."

"Weird and wacky," Joey whispered. "Dottie thinks she's psychic."

"Oh," Allie said softly. It was strange that a girl as perfect as Jessa had a mother like that.

They walked together toward the path and underneath the bridge, keeping quiet so they could hear any possible shouts for help. Occasionally, they called Tulip's name, but all they heard was the distant whoosh of the ocean, birds chirping, and a soft wind rustling through the trees and saw palmettos. Allie hadn't actually been too worried until that moment. What if they didn't find Tulip before nightfall?

"Are there alligators here?" she whispered.

Joey nodded. "You wanna know how to tell if there's an alligator in the water?"

She nodded.

"It's wet."

"The water is wet?" It took her a second to clue in. "Oh, you're saying they're everywhere." She shivered and scanned the top of the water for bugging eyes watching them. Alligators were one thing they most certainly did not have in Nashville.

Joey moved a branch from the path and waited for her to pass before releasing it to snap back. "But you know what the most dangerous animal is, right?"

"Coyotes? Bears?"

"Humans."

Even though he was clearly enjoying freaking her out, the word still stabbed like a knife. It was the first time it occurred to her that something really, really bad might actually have happened to the awkward young girl she'd met on her front porch—the lanky teen with a terrible bowl-shaped haircut who hid behind Jessa. What if she wasn't alone? What if something truly awful had happened to her? Allie shivered. What if it was happening right now?

She picked up her pace, and Joey followed. Soon, she was running full out, scanning the woods for a view of the lighthouse or a white birch tree. She didn't know what she would do if she found Tulip with some sort of human or reptilian monster, aside from scream as loudly as she could. But at least that was something—at least Tulip wouldn't be alone.

Finally, she heard the faraway sirens of the local sheriff—hopefully, they were flying down the tiny asphalt road at top speed. It felt like every passing second brought them closer to doom. "Tulip!" she yelled, panic and urgency in her voice. She struggled to keep up the pace with so many sticks and weeds on the path, but she was a runner, she could do it.

A loud bark answered her. "Cuppie!" she called, stopping so she could hear better. "Sam?"

Cuppie ran straight for her at full speed, fur flying and mouth open. As soon as she got to Allie and Joey, she made a full circle around them before heading back the way she came. "You want us to follow you? Good girl," Allie said as they all fell into step. "Sam!" she yelled again.

"Up ahead!" he answered. "I've got her!"

Sam came into view carrying a soaking wet girl. "Is she okay?" Allie asked as she caught up to him.

Tulip smiled despite the tears running down her dirt-streaked face as Sam answered, "Broken ankle." Allie heard the strain in his voice and noticed the tilt of Tulip's body. Sam was barely able to hold her legs aloft with his injured left arm.

"We were so worried," Allie said. She put her arms underneath Tulip's legs. Sam shifted, allowing her to share the load.

Mud covered Tulip's jeans and purple shirt. "Mama's gonna have my hide."

"Most of all," Allie said, "she's going to be so, so happy that you're alive."

"Yeah." Tulip had one hand on her belly, and it looked like there was something big underneath it. "I got one," she said when she noticed Allie looking.

"A shark tooth?"

She nodded. "Megalodon," she said and held up a large black tooth twice the size of her hand. "It's thirty million years old." She sniffed deeply. "I got a thresher and an orange tiger too." In the arm she had around Sam's neck, she opened her fist to show two tiny, pointy versions of the huge triangular tooth.

"I texted the group. They're coming," Joey said, taking his eyes off his phone long enough to notice Allie and Sam smashed together, holding Tulip. "I can carry her," he said.

Allie felt Sam stiffen. She knew he didn't want to give up carrying Tulip. "We've got her," she said. "You want to go on ahead and help guide them in?"

Joey frowned, but he did as he was told.

"Nice guy," Sam said.

His words didn't sound genuine. They sounded jealous.

"Joey works with my sister," Tulip said. "He makes good spaghetti." She flinched. "I'm hungry."

"We'll get you something to eat as soon as we can," Allie said.

"Can I pet your dog when we get back to camp?" Tulip asked. "She found me."

"She did," Sam agreed. "Buttercup's got a good nose, and she especially loves scratches on her head and under her collar."

Tulip's voice went high-pitched, outside of the softened fearful and pained tone from just a second ago. "Want some scratchies, old girl?"

"Goll dang it, Tulip!" Dottie's voice bellowed from the path ahead.

"I'm sorry, Mama," she yelled. "I slipped in the mud."

Fred followed behind her, fast-walking with a toothpick in his mouth and the coat of his Santa suit unbuttoned and flapping behind him.

"Hey, Uncle Fred!" At the sight of him, Tulip burst into tears.

He ran up and gently took her from Sam and Allie. "You okay, sweetheart?" He kissed her on the head, and she nuzzled into his neck, looking more like a little girl than ever. "You scared us something fierce."

"My ankle hurts."

"It looks like it does," he said.

"Don't be too nice to her, Dewayne," Dottie said. "She's in trouble."

"She can be in trouble later."

"Did you see where I was, Mama?" Tulip asked.

"I did."

Fresh tears streamed down her face. "And you sent the dog to find me?"

"No, that guy did." Dottie pointed at Sam before leaning in to hold her daughter's face. She planted an aggressive kiss firmly on her forehead.

Jessa and Duke walked up together. She'd clearly hung behind to stay with the older, slower man. Jessa was nice like that. "Don't ever do that again, Tootie!" she said. "You know I can't live without you."

"It's like you always say about asking for help," Tulip said to Jessa as her big sister smothered her face with kisses.

"That's right, darlin'," Jessa said. "You've got to have your people."

"It took all of us to find you," Sam said.

It was a strange feeling for Allie to be a part of that group, even if only temporarily. They were tight. They were each other's go-to, their backup, and their first call. How nice it must be.

The crowd moved together toward the camp, and Allie tried to walk anywhere but alongside Joey or Sam. Tulip chatted and held tight to her uncle Fred the whole way. "Jess, did you get my phone from school?"

"No, she did not," Dottie answered for her. "And don't you plan on seeing that phone for a while now, ya hear?"

"Mama!" The tears started all over again, but this time much louder.

Chapter Seven

ALLIE SAT ON the back porch, staring through the trees at the shimmering salt marsh. It was mesmerizing, like tiny twinkle lights strewn across a watery field. To the far right she caught a glimpse of the lighthouse. She knew what was out there now—an old camp, a creek filled with fossils, a beach, a trail through the woods, and lifetimes of memories for the people who camped there. Allie's childhood had never been the summer camp sort. There was no time for that. She'd made commitments to her gymnastics team, her dance team, and her charity work. At least, that was the household mantra: *You make a commitment, you stick to it.*

But the truth was, her mother made those commitments on her behalf. Allie just did the work, suffered the injuries, won the medals, and still managed to get a certificate every year for never missing a day of school. That certificate also belonged to her mother. Allie wasn't mad about it. She knew she had those buzzwords she saw all over social media—words like *resilience* and *grit*. She knew she was capable, and she knew how to work hard too. But summer camp, even just once, would've been nice.

She pulled her cold feet onto the chair and tucked her knit blanket around them. The moon was busy overpowering the sun, casting melon colors across the sky. If only it was summertime, she might see some fireflies. "Dad?" she breathed. "Why?" Why hadn't he been more present in her life? Why had he left her mother to handle everything? He was more than just a paycheck, he was more than the roof over their heads. But he didn't know it. He was a great protector, and a good provider, but he'd missed out on being a friend. Now it was too late.

The scene of Sam struggling to keep hold of Tulip switched back and forth in her mind from Sam to her father. She could still feel the strength in her dad's arms as he spun her around or hugged her tight. She would never have that again. Never feel safe in that way again.

Then there was Sam, using every muscle in his body to compensate for his weak left arm—she'd seen the strain in his face and neck. He would have torn a muscle before he dropped that little girl. Allie softened more toward him, and that was dangerous. She tossed aside the warm feeling and forced herself to be realistic. Sam was incapable of apologizing. And he, apparently, had plenty of chicks she would soon have the displeasure of sharing her space with. He was a wounded soldier, a traumatized soul, and a man who should probably rescue all of the scary dogs and live alone with them for the rest of his life.

A squirrel ran down a nearby tree and up another, and

Allie wondered if squirrels had mates for life. She hoped they did.

Now, she thought, *enough of Sam*. She needed to process her feelings for Joey. She used her thumb to tap each finger—one, two, three, four, four, three, two, one. Then she called up his image, remembering the events of the day. Joey working behind Fred's counter, communicating with the group, staying by her side as they searched. Was it possible that she only liked him because she had some sort of unresolved heartbreak from her ex? He looked only about 40 percent like him, and their personalities were completely different. He was not Mark. And that was good. She didn't even want Mark anymore. And it wasn't fair to have feelings for Joey just because he reminded her of someone who'd left her. Getting Joey to love her wasn't going to fix that pain of abandonment. There were no do-overs in life. Plus, he was her coworker. And this was her dream job. She would be the dumbest girl on the planet if she screwed it up by trying to force a romance.

She plopped her feet to the floor in exasperation. Why was she even thinking about this? She did not need a man in her life! And she needed to stop battling with her own brain. "Suck it up, Allie," she told herself. "You're good enough the way you are. You're just fine alone."

She gathered up her soft blanket and tapped her toe twice on the threshold before entering the house. Cuppie was curled up next to a fire, and Sam was at the kitchen table.

"It's cold out there," she said.

"Yeah," he answered. "I built you a fire."

The fire was for her? "Thanks." She sat on the hearth and put her freezing toes as close as she could to the warmth.

"Did you see that Tulip's home?" he asked.

"No, I left my phone in my room."

"The bones weren't misaligned, so the doctors put her in a boot."

"It's nice that you're an EMT, and that you knew what to do when you found her. It could have been so much worse," she said. He had a pile of sticks in front of him that he appeared to be snipping and tying together with twine. "What are you doing?"

"Making a Christmas decoration." He chuckled. "I'm hoping it looks like a tree when I'm done."

She wished he would stop being so excited about Christmas.

Cuppie's head jerked up, her ears alerted to the front door. Seconds later, there was a knock. Sam immediately stood to get it, with Cuppie leading the way.

It was Tulip and Jessa. Apparently, the Boone family had no problem with consistently dropping by unannounced.

"Sam!" Tulip declared, stumbling into the house on crutches. Buttercup didn't try to intervene, she just wagged excitedly. Jessa grabbed Tulip's crutches as Sam picked her up in a long one-armed hug and swung her over to the kitchen. He tried to set her down on a pulled out chair, but she stayed glued to his side, her head stuffed into his armpit. Allie couldn't help but smile. It was obvious that Tulip Boone had developed a crush.

"Sorry, y'all!" Jessa said. "Tootie has something she wants to give to Sam."

Suddenly filled with shyness, Tulip left his side long enough to stuff her hand in the pocket of her pink sweatpants and pull out a leather cord with a shark tooth tied to the end. She held it up to him. "It's the tiger shark tooth," she said. "The one I found in the creek today."

Sam seemed genuinely touched. He pulled her into his side again. "Can you put it on me?" He sat in the chair, and she hopped on one foot to the spot behind him.

"Tiger sharks are the only sharks that don't have taste buds," she explained. "A great white or a bull shark might take a chunk, but then they're gonna let you go. They think humans taste nasty. But a tiger shark is the most dangerous because it's gonna eat every last bit, right down to your fingernails. People don't normally survive tiger shark attacks."

"That is an awesome piece of trivia." Sam chuckled as she tied the cord into several knots behind his neck. "And you are super smart."

"Yeah." She blushed. "Mama chose our daddies because she wanted me to be smart and she wanted Jessa to be beautiful."

Jessa smiled and laughingly agreed with the statement,

but to Allie, it felt like the air in the room suddenly vibrated.

"We've never met them," Tulip added as if it were a normal thing to say.

Sam's eyes were on Jessa, probably to judge how he should react before saying, "Well, she did a good job getting exactly what she wanted. Except that I think you're both smart and beautiful."

Jessa looked away as Tulip turned red from the neck up. Sam, wearing his prehistoric shark tooth necklace, stood for a third hug. "Thank you," he said, squeezing her tight.

"Okay, y'all!" Jessa reverted back to her peppy self. "We're gonna let you enjoy your evening. Toot's got to get ready for school tomorrow, and the morning's gonna come early. Thank y'all again for your help today."

"Yeah, thanks," Tulip said, clearly not wishing to extricate herself from Sam. He picked her up again and glided her along, her feet just inches off the floor, down the front steps to the passenger side of Jessa's car. She opened the door, and he gently placed Tulip on the seat. When the car was out of sight, he met Allie on the front porch, his hand wrapped around the pointy tooth on his new necklace.

"I might never take this thing off," he said.

She was touched that he appreciated it so much. "It's your reward for being a hero."

"I'm no hero." His pitch changed, like her words just hit a soft spot. "If you need more logs for the fire, I stacked some wood outside by the porch." He turned to leave, and she almost asked him to stay. She wanted to talk about what Tulip had just said. Wasn't it shocking? Wouldn't knowing that your mother slept with some man because she wanted a designer baby mess with a person's head? And did the men even know they had daughters? There was so much to question.

Sam patted his thigh, and together he and Buttercup walked toward the bedroom. "Good night," he said without looking back.

"Good night." At least, it used to be a good night. Inadvertently, she had tapped into something deep within him. Something dark.

Chapter Eight

"WHAT A WEEK!" Joey said, handing Allie a paper cup of coffee from Fred's. "Are you staying for the show tonight?"

Every Friday night was Music among the Vines at the Saltwater Winery. A band was scheduled to play, and crowds from as far north as Isle of Palms and south as St. Helena flocked to tiny Goose Island. That Friday was Carolina Beach Music, which, in the Lowcountry, meant guests would be swinging and swaying to old tunes from The Embers, Jackie Williams, and Caribbean Cowboys. To be honest, Allie hadn't yet decided if she was staying. "Are you?" she asked, not sure what she hoped his answer would be.

"Oh, yeah. Jessa and Libby too. Dottie's bringing the truck. It's gonna be a good time."

Allie immediately recognized that her three closest work friends had made plans without her. It shook her confidence. Had she done something to make them dislike her? "I mean," she began, "I wish I'd worn a cuter outfit."

"Oh, come on now. You always look great." Joey said it so easily, she couldn't tell if he meant it or not. The fuzzy yellow sweater she wore was comfortable, but all day long she'd felt like a bumblebee, since she made the mistake of pairing it with black pants. He sat in his chair and squeaked it around to face his desk. Discussion over.

She quietly tapped her hand on her thigh in sequences of four. She hadn't done something fun on a Friday night in ages. What were her other options? Go home and hide out in her room to avoid Sam and Cuppie? Drive to Charleston and get a hotel room where she could be miserable and alone? Part of her wanted to drive the nine hours back to Nashville just for some familiarity. She had tons of friends she could meet up with there. A fancy cocktail at a local off-Broadway bar sounded better than it ever had before. Her mother's word reverberated in her head. *Cherophobia*. It really pissed her off. She did not have an irrational aversion to being happy. She knew full well that being happy would not cause something bad to happen. She'd been happy plenty of times. Most of her life, actually. Just not recently. Just not since the death of her dad. The white of her computer screen faded to a fuzzy gray as she realized that she was still tapping on her leg. Why was she tapping? Because she felt strongly that if she didn't, she would be responsible for bringing about something terrible. Well, you know what? Her dad was dead. So clearly, bad things happened anyway.

She stopped tapping. "I'm going," she said more loudly than she meant to.

"Alright!" Joey seemed genuinely pleased. "Jessa said

Dottie's doing fried shrimp and chicken. French fries, too, I think. We'll probably sell a bunch of the dry white to pair with it. It oughta be good."

"I'm really happy. It sounds great," Allie said, feeling like she had to say the word *happy* out loud, and noting how fake she sounded. "Happy, happy, happy," she added with as much oomph as she could muster. She sounded like a kindergartner, but Joey didn't seem to mind.

He chuckled as he mocked her. "We're all gonna be happy, happy, happy, and drunk, drunk, drunk."

She giggled in reply. She hadn't been drunk, drunk, drunk in ages. Maybe it was time.

It ended up being the slowest day she'd had so far. Fridays at the winery had an air of fun that made the work feel like drudgery. She still had to finish testing samples to decide when to disgorge the yeast from the new sparkling wines that were currently in the riddling machine, but she'd much rather be hanging out with the guests underneath the oaks with a finished glass of wine in her hand. She had to force herself to remember why she was there. She'd worked hard to earn her expertise, she was building her career, and she wasn't going to let a stupid desire for fun interfere.

It was Jessa who finally sounded the "weekend is here" alarm. "Woooooohoooo!" she sang, skipping down the hallway. "Who wants to help me put the goats away?"

Libby was directly behind her, her strawberry-blond hair as puffy as her pink sleeves. "Skip's an asshole," she said. "He chewed the tassel off my purse."

"Why'd you get your purse so close to him?" Jessa asked. "He's a *goat*, Libs. They eat everything."

"I'll help," Joey said. "Allie, you want to lure the chickens to the coop?"

As fun as luring chickens sounded, she was still working on the analysis. "I'll meet y'all out there in a bit. I've got to finish this up."

Joey leaned in and looked at her computer. "That can wait until Monday."

"I'll feel better if I finish it." She couldn't imagine leaving it over the weekend; she would obsess about it the whole time.

His dark brow furrowed, but he recovered quickly and left with Jessa and Libby. Allie stared at her screen, trying to reengage her concentration, but a big part of her felt like she'd just made a mistake. How was she going to make friends if she didn't join in when they wanted her to? Then again, they were just putting the animals away. And she was going to stay for the band. It would be okay, she told herself. She'd allow herself to get a little tipsy, and that would loosen her up. "Happy, happy, happy," she whispered to herself. "Drunk, drunk, drunk."

Dottie's food truck was decorated with Christmas lights, and she'd even tied a huge blow-up Santa to the top. "Come here," she yelled at Allie as she walked by. Allie jogged up to the window, stopping to say hi to Tulip, who was busy putting bottled water into a half wine barrel filled with ice. "Now, listen," Dottie said. "You need to stop trying so hard. You're like an old woman who doesn't eat her fiber, you're so blocked up."

Allie immediately thought back to her last bathroom visit.

"Don't be stupid," Dottie said like she could read her mind. "You're blocking out all the good 'cause you're focusing on the wrong things."

"I'm just trying to do the best job I can."

"Naw, it's more than that." Dottie reached through the window and motioned for Allie to hold her hand. It was warm and calloused. "Honey, you can't make an omelet without breaking a leg."

Did she mean egg? Maybe she had said egg, and Allie was just distracted by Dottie's missing bottom tooth so close to her face.

"Everything costs something," Dottie went on. "There will always be things that suck in our lives. So just accept it and enjoy the good things that come your way."

That was no big revelation for Allie. An Instagram video could have told her that. Gratitude was the key to happiness. She'd been told that her whole life. She tried to pull her hand away, but Dottie held tight.

"You got a big ol' firewall built up. Did somebody break your heart?"

Allie felt like she should say Mark, because he did break

her heart. But the real answer was *my dad*. And then *my mom*. She tore her hand from Dottie's. "Thanks for the advice," she said, not meaning it at all.

"Hey," Tulip called out as she walked away. "Is Sam coming tonight?"

Allie shook her head. "Don't think so."

"You should invite him," she said brightly, looking adorable with her bad haircut in a tiny ponytail and a Christmas green sweatshirt that matched her eyes.

Allie gave her a thumbs-up. She had no intention of inviting Sam, no matter how much she was softening toward him. This was her night to really get to know Joey.

One wine bottle was supposed to serve four people, but with the way Libby poured, they had to open two. It was no big deal; they had an unlimited supply from the tasting room. Joey was right. The dry white wine went perfectly with Dottie's fried shrimp, chicken, coleslaw, and French fries. Allie felt free to drink it like water with her meal.

The sun was low when the stage lights flicked on and the band's guitarist woke up the night with a catchy tune. The smile on Allie's face felt as big as the rising moon. *Happy, happy, happy.* The group sat together at a picnic table far enough away that they could still talk over the music. Libby droned on and on about her wedding plans. She was in the early stages of planning and had hundreds of photos of old barns outfitted with chandeliers and tulle swags. "I'm hitting up all of the thrift stores for people's old china so that each guest can take home a place setting as a wedding favor," she said.

Allie's imagination was alight with the idea. "That sounds like so much fun! I'd love to help you look!"

Libby gave her the side-eye, saying nothing.

Instantly, the old feelings of inadequacy slammed back into her. How very short-lived happiness was. Why didn't Libby like her?

"We should all go!" Jessa said. "We can be the Three Saltwater Thrifters. Isn't that cute?"

"Totally!" Libby agreed, looking only at Jessa. "I'm looking for crystal glasses too. But they're harder to find."

Allie pasted on an artificial smile. What had just happened? "What a great idea!" she said, feigning excitement. "So creative."

"Right?" Libby smiled graciously.

"You mean the Four Saltwater Thrifters, right?" Joey made a hurt face.

"You want to come?" Jessa asked.

"No, but y'all should invite me just to be nice."

"You're invited," Libby said.

"Good." He smirked. "But that sounds more boring than Duke's three-hour staff meetings. So, no."

Allie poured herself another glass of wine. She was going to need to tread carefully with Libby. She seemed like the type to cause drama. "Does Duke come to these Friday night shows?"

"Duke's been like a hermit since his wife died," Jessa said. "He hides as much as he can." She jumped up, suddenly full of energy. "C'mon, Joey. Let's dance!"

Just like that, Allie was left alone with Libby. She took a big sip from her wineglass and tried to think of something to talk about. "It sure is nice out here," she said. "Warm enough that we don't really need the big heaters."

Libby gave her a weak smile, merely acknowledging that Allie had said something.

"And the band is really good. We don't hear much of this kind of music in Nashville."

Libby cut her eyes at her, her smile smaller than before.

Tall, thin Joey and beautiful Jessa danced like they'd been taking lessons their whole lives, spinning and dipping with shuffles in between. Allie felt pangs of jealousy and immediately went to work suppressing them by tapping her fingernails as quickly as she could on the wooden table—four, three, two, one, one, two, three, four, repeat, repeat, repeat.

"Oh my God," Libby snapped. "Will you stop that? It is so annoying."

Allie felt herself flush. "Sorry." She picked up her wineglass and took a big swig.

Libby huffed and stood, throwing words at Allie like charity. "I'm going to the restroom."

Happy, happy, happy, Allie thought to herself while staring at Joey and Jessa. *Happy, happy, happy.* She drained her glass and poured some more. Her nose was numb, but her chest was beginning to loosen and her brain was blooming like a morning glory in the sunshine. She was letting go of the firewall Dottie spoke of, letting go of the curse of caring too much what people thought of her. By the time Joey and Jessa finally sat back down with her, she was sweetly relaxed.

"Libby went to the bathroom," she said. "Y'all are such good dancers." Had she just said *dan-shers*? Whatever. Joey sat on the bench next to her, and she scooted closer to him. Jessa looked at her strangely. Or did she? Allie wasn't sure.

"You know what?" Jessa said. "I think I'm gonna head on home. I'm sure Mama needs me to feed the cats since she and Toots are working tonight. The little monsters are probably tearing up the place."

"Awwww," Allie said. "That's sho shweet. I love kitty catsh." Had she always had a lisp? Her tongue felt like it would horribly fail a roadside sobriety test.

"Do you want a ride home?" Jessa asked her. "It's no problem at all."

"Nope." Allie brazenly rested her head on Joey's shoulder. She was definitely staying right where she was.

Chapter Nine

ALLIE WAS GOING to kiss Joey. As soon as she saw a chance, she would just lean on in and plant one on his very Mark-like lips. The lips that were currently moving around as they said something incomprehensible to her. Kissing someone was not a big deal. It was a test. A foolproof way to know if there were sparks. *Happy, happy, happy.* The words in her head were now set to the swinging tune of the band as she stood and wiggled next to the picnic table. Her dancing was exceptionally good, she could feel it. People were probably watching and thinking how impressed they were with her tight grasp of rhythm and her unique moves. She twirled and tripped over a tree root. It wasn't a bad fall, so she got up and kept grooving.

Happy, happy, happy, dance, dance, dance, drunk, drunk, drunk. God, the band was good. How did those people get their instruments to play the right notes at the right time? It was genius! Musicians were such amazingly talented humans. She could kiss all of them. Even the gross one with the long beard. She laughed out loud. "Joey!" she called. He had spun away from her and was talking to Libby. "Joey! Come here and kiss me!" She laughed as she shuffled her feet and swung her hips.

He came toward her, but he brought Libby with him. "Allie, Libby will be driving you home tonight."

"I want you to drive me home, Joey!" She meant to step forward and reach for his hand, but instead fell onto him. Thankfully, he caught her.

"That would not look good for either of us," he said sternly. "Libby will take you home."

"I don't like Libby," she said with her face smashed into his chest.

"Well," Joey said like he was highly annoyed with her. "She doesn't like you either."

Allie righted herself and tried to focus on her surroundings. "I'm not riding with her." She squinted at Libby's face all tight with judgment and superiority. "I'm not riding with you." Dottie's yellow truck with the bright Christmas lights caught her eye. "Dottie can take me home. She's my neighbor."

Joey sighed loudly before thanking Libby and saying something about making sure it was okay with Dottie. He sat Allie at the picnic table and left.

"Screw them," Allie said under her breath. She didn't have to do anything they said. She stood and followed him to Dottie's truck.

"Allie-girl," Dottie yelled. "You been overserved?"

Allie nodded, grateful to have made it to the truck. She

leaned against it, shooting the meanest face she could muster at Joey.

"We've got an hour of cleanup, and then we'll go," Dottie said. "Stay where I can see you."

What was she, a child? Her mother used to say the same thing. "Okay," Allie answered, knowing full well she would do no such thing. "I'm not going to bed tonight," Allie informed Dottie. "I'm not tired."

"Well, we'll just cross that bitch when we come to it now, won't we?" Dottie said.

Allie was somewhat sure Dottie meant cross that *bridge*, although crossing a bitch sounded really, really good.

"Thanks for getting her home safely, Dottie," said Joey, the prude traitor. "Allie, I'll see you Monday."

"See you Monday," she mocked him before turning back to Dottie. "Joey won't kiss me, he won't even freaking drive me home, but he'll see me Monday." It felt like Mark abandoning her all over again. It felt like her dad dying and never, ever coming back. Why wouldn't men do what she wanted? What was wrong with her?

Joey ignored her and walked away. If she had been able to bend down and successfully stand back up, she would've thrown a rock at him. Dottie was deep in the truck, back at work, so Allie took the opportunity to skedaddle out of there. If she snuck through the vineyard, no one would see her. She was smart enough not to drive, but she could darn well get herself home using her own two feet.

It was hard not to laugh out loud as she ran through the vineyard in her black ballet flats, with the moon as her only source of light. It was chilly, but the wind in her hair felt fabulous. She tried to do a split leap like she used to back in her childhood ballet class. She was a lord a-leaping. How many of them were there in that Christmas song? Ten? Or was that ladies dancing? She spun around and stopped when she got dizzy. She had to bend down and hold on to her knees until she caught her breath. When she stood back up, she sang as loudly as she could, "Five golden rings." Then she ran again, picking up the pace.

"Four calling birds, three French hens, two turtle doves"—she stopped and spread her arms out wide—"and a partridge in a pear tree." It was hard to run in a straight line between the prickly vines. She kept scraping her arms by swerving when she didn't mean to. She needed more room than the pathway offered, so at her first chance, she pivoted left and made her way to the main road with the plan of hiding if any cars or big yellow food trucks drove by. She loved how fit she was, and the fact that she could run for miles. Not everybody could do that. She focused on the strike of her foot, the length of her stride, and her posture. She looked good, she knew she did, just like when she was dancing.

Wait. She stopped, suddenly assaulted with the memory of falling back at the winery. Had she tripped on a tree root and fallen? *Oh, no.* Had Joey seen her? The late stages of her evening began to come into view. Her body must be metabolizing the alcohol, her liver working hard, the French fries she barely remembered eating probably helping by closing the valve at the bottom of her stomach for digestion and thereby keeping the remaining alcohol from absorbing into her intestines as quickly.

It took at least one hour to process each drink. How many glasses of... *Oh, no.* Her mouth fell open when she remembered telling Joey to kiss her. And, *oh, Lord*, she'd told Libby she didn't like her. Allie looked down at her black dress pants and yellow sweater. She was out in the wilderness running in her work clothes. No, she did not look good. Nothing about her evening had been good. There was no *happy, happy, happy*. There was only *drunk, drunk, drunk*. Her stomach churned, and she knew what was coming. She leaned over the nearest bush and vomited a stomach full of liquid. Stumbling, she made it to a giant oak tree and used the ground as a seat and the trunk as the back of her nature-chair. She promptly fell asleep.

The moon was hidden behind dark clouds when she awoke, still living her nightmare. It was hard to tell which direction to walk in the pitch dark, but at least she had the road to follow. It would get her somewhere. She didn't have her purse or her cell phone. Maybe they were still at her desk. She wanted to cry. Why was she so stupid?

There was a dim light up ahead, and she hoped it was Fred's gas station. She had no idea what time it was. Maybe it was still open and she could sit for a minute and have some water. He could call Dottie for her too. Someone needed to tell her neighbor not to worry.

But as she came upon the building, it was obvious it'd been closed for a while. The only light came from the masthead on Fred's grounded houseboat. Should she bother him? Was this enough of an emergency to wake someone she barely knew from what she presumed was a sound sleep? She rambled over the gravel parking lot to the graying picnic table and plopped down with a loud squeak. Immediately, Fred's dog started barking. Whiskey barked for several minutes until a light at the back of the boat flicked on, and Fred appeared with a flashlight. She braced herself for discovery.

Whiskey got to her first, screeching to a stop once he found her. "Hey, boy," she said. "It's okay. Just me." Either the dog remembered her or sensed she wasn't a threat, because he stopped barking immediately. "Hi, Fred," she called out. "It's just me, Allie Westley."

"You alright?" he asked, shining the flashlight at her.

"Yeah. Just walking home."

"Dottie's out at the winery looking for you. I'm gonna call her."

She could barely see him, but she did notice that his beard was brown instead of white. He must spray it with something when he dressed up like Santa. He hung up the phone after filling in Dottie, and sat across from her. "Listen,

I worked over twenty years as a corporate lawyer, and I'm good at keeping secrets, so you don't need to worry about me tellin' anyone."

Did the gas station owner just say *corporate lawyer*? "I thought you were Dottie's brother," Allie said.

"I am. I'm also a Harvard grad."

It took a minute to sink in. How did toothless Dottie have a brother who was a lawyer? Harvard? This was Tulip and Jessa's uncle? Allie felt like she was in an alternate universe.

"People aren't always what they seem," he said.

She'd heard that said before, but it never meant as much as in that moment. "Yeah, and I hope the people realize that the drunk person they saw tonight is not the real me."

"Some will know, and some won't."

Allie put her head in her hands. "I'm so embarrassed. And I'm so sorry for waking you up. I don't even know what time it is."

"It's not too late." He checked his phone. "Comin' up on midnight. You need a ride home?"

"Yeah, I think I do."

She climbed up into his old red pickup truck and slid onto the torn bench seat, finding herself in awe once again. This man had been a lawyer? "Can I ask why you're not a lawyer anymore?"

"Because a smart person is a surgeon of the mind."

She had no idea what that meant and couldn't think of

an intelligent response. Thankfully, he spoke again.

"I wasn't happy," he said, waiting for Whiskey to jump in before he got behind the wheel.

"I know what that feels like," she whispered, putting her hand on Whiskey's back as he sat in the middle of them.

"I wanted a calm life and a kind one," he went on, starting up the truck with a roar. "See, there are two ways of being rich. Either you can increase the amount of money you make or you can decrease the kinds of things you want. All of the money I had wasn't making me happy—it was doing the opposite. So, I worked on my mind. I cut out the parts that didn't serve me, and here I am."

"You wanted a simpler way of life?" Allie tried to distill what he was saying down to something easily understood.

"No, I wanted a richer way of life. It's not simple at all."

Maybe there wasn't an easy answer to big life questions. "So, more meaningful?"

"Yes. And, for me, that means being around people. I try not to guess their intentions or have expectations of them. I just accept them how they are."

"That sounds impossible."

"Sometimes it is."

They hit a pothole, and Allie's head brushed the ceiling. "But what if people are awful?"

"Serial killer awful? Are we talking evil? Or just your average, everyday awful?"

Allie thought about Libby's pinched face and didn't want to admit that the woman was probably everyday awful but not actually evil. "Average, I guess."

"Well, it's not your job to fix them, so just love them from a distance."

"And hope they change?"

"Don't have the expectation that they will ever change. Just know that you hold the power because you get to decide if you will have a relationship with them or not."

"Well, I don't think I'm going to be loving this person or having a relationship with her. But I have to see her at work every day."

"Then maybe just try to understand her."

She looked past Whiskey to Fred's bearded face and messy hair. He had wrinkles by his eyes from years of smiling, and a look of strength about him despite his thin frame. There he was in faded plaid pajama pants and an old NEW YORK YANKEES T-shirt, counseling her and driving her home at midnight. Gas station Fred was so much more than she'd ever considered. How many other people did she think she knew when, in fact, she was completely wrong?

They pulled up to her little cottage, and all the lights were on. Sam and Cuppie stood on the front porch. Sam was dressed in sweats and running shoes, and Cuppie was all leashed up like they were about to go for a walk. Allie knew she'd just been caught. They were clearly about to go out searching for her.

Embarrassment spread from her chest, up her neck, and settled like a burn on her face. How much worse could one night get?

Chapter Ten

ALLIE DIDN'T FEEL like talking. What was there to say? She didn't owe Sam an explanation. He was her roommate, not her father. She walked past him on the front porch and went straight to her room. She didn't even acknowledge Cuppie despite the happy wagging and nose nudge to her thigh. Her life was no one's business but her own.

She shut the door to her room and locked it. A shower would be nice, but there was no way she would risk seeing Sam in the hallway. Sam with his fake look of worry, Sam with his *never made a mistake in my life* perfection. So, he had act-it-out nightmares. Whatever. At least he wasn't getting drunk at his place of employment and hitting on his coworker.

Allie felt like calling her mother, but her phone was still somewhere at the winery. Usually, it was anger that stopped her from calling. Now she couldn't call her even though she finally wanted to. Anyway, her mother was probably sound asleep with the random man she'd been dating. Truthfully, the late hour didn't matter—all through college Allie called her mother whenever she needed her, and her mother always answered. It was the man part Allie struggled with. It was so disrespectful of her. Disrespectful of the family they'd had when her dad was alive. She sat on the edge of her bed, filled with regret and exhaustion. She might still be a little drunk too. It was all she could do to get her shoes off before the soft bed consumed her like a cottony cloud, and she promptly passed out.

Morning was not welcome. She didn't know whether it was the smell of bacon or the loud clap of thunder that woke her up, but she wished it hadn't. If only she could sleep for the rest of her life, she wouldn't have to face the fact that she'd made an idiot of herself. But as hard as she tried to fall back into oblivion, there was no denying that she desperately had to pee or that she was still wearing the black and yellow bumblebee outfit from the day before. She opened her door as quietly as she could and tiptoed down the hall to the bathroom. Just as she got to the door, Sam walked around the corner.

"Hey, you want some breakfast? It's gonna get nasty out there today. Thought I'd make something warm."

Allie froze, her hand on the bathroom doorknob, one step away from privacy and much-needed relief. "No, thanks."

"Well, I'll save you some in case you change your mind."

She practically dove into the bathroom and locked the door behind her. Why, why, why did her roommate have to keep including her? They were not friends. They were just two people who happened to share a house. They should be ignoring each other. She leaned against the door and looked around the tiny, functional space. First, she needed the toilet, which was the only thing that actually felt good that morning. Then she had to brush her disgusting teeth, and shower her scraped-up, filthy, dehydrated body. It was torture to be inside her brain at the moment. She'd never been so angry at herself.

She went to tap the faucet three times with her pinky finger before she turned it on. Screw that, she thought. Screw the taps. What were they saving her from? Nothing. If something bad was going to happen, let it. She wanted to scream out, *LET IT!* She turned the faucet on full blast, brushed her teeth, and got in the shower, denying herself the option to go back for the taps. *Bring it on, universe.* She didn't even wait for the required two drips on her nose from the disengaged showerhead before she allowed herself to exit. She just got out of the shower, clean and pissed enough to let whatever was going to happen happen.

She'd forgotten to bring fresh clothes to the bathroom, so she sprinted in her towel to her bedroom. Whatever Sam was cooking smelled like heaven. Her stomach growled, and she was dying for some water. A loud clap of thunder shook the house. At least the weather matched her mood. She put her wet hair in a bun and slipped on her old sweatpants and MUSIC CITY sweatshirt. You know what? She needed food, there was some freshly made in the kitchen, and dammit, she was going to eat it. She stomped to the kitchen like the leader of a marching band and took a glass from the cupboard. Sam was eating at the kitchen table, and Cuppie was watching her every move from in front of the fireplace. Without a word, Allie chugged a full glass of water.

"Does the breakfast offer still stand?" she asked, catching her breath.

"Of course. I made enough for both of us." He was so engrossed in his phone that he barely paid attention to her, which was nice.

She filled her plate with bacon, sausage, and some sort of egg scramble made with bell peppers, onions, and cheese. High protein, just like she'd expect from someone with muscles like his. When she sat at the table with him, she noticed he had Christmas music softly playing. Adding Christmas music to her current mental state felt like gasoline on a fire. "Please turn that music off," she said, trying to sound calm.

He laughed. "What do you have against Christmas?"

"I told you, I'm skipping the traditional stuff this year." She stuffed a forkful of eggs into her mouth before a curse word came out. He didn't deserve her anger. It should all be aimed at herself, and yet it was absolutely, 100 percent, about to come out sideways. "Thank you for the food." She attempted to have the decency to feel bad about her attitude toward him. Or maybe it was her attitude toward her mother and all the expectations for Christmas. But there was no decency left in her.

Her thoughts were everywhere. Christmas. Big mistakes. Joey. Libby. Jessa. Dottie. Fred. Sam. She owed many apologies, but most would have to wait until Monday. She took another bite, watching Sam from the corner of her eye. He was leaving her alone, his dog now snoozing peacefully in front of the bright fire. The house felt cozy, and his food was beginning to help her feel human again. What had she learned from Fred the night before? People weren't always what they seemed. The truth was, she had no idea who Sam was. She took a deep breath, and tried to recover her old sense of self.

"This is really good," she said.

He briefly looked up from his phone. "Glad you like it."

She ate some more. "So, do you have plans for Christmas?"

He put the phone down. "I was hoping to talk to you about that."

Uh-oh. She braced herself. He was going to ask to have people over. She could sense it. Maybe he had a girlfriend?

"My old commanding officer is going to be in Charleston for the holidays. He's older and kind of like a mentor to me. His wife died about ten years back, and he's a really good guy. I'd like to have him over. If it's okay with you, of course."

Did he really think she'd say no to a widower? "Sure. I

was planning to go someplace else anyway."

"You don't need to go anywhere," he said. "You can join us."

She had a date with the beach, a sandwich, and a nap. "No, thanks." Christmas was exactly a week away. That meant that the three-year anniversary of her dad's death was in just four days.

The way Sam kept looking at her felt like he had something else to say. It was almost like he could read her thoughts. An intense feeling of vulnerability washed over her like a flash flood. She pushed her plate away and got up from the table. She needed touch, affection, and connection, and she hated that. But some healthy part of her walked over to Cuppie, got down on the floor, and gently put her hands in the dog's soft gray fur. Cuppie craned her neck to see who it was before plopping her head back where it'd been. Allie scratched and stroked from the dog's head to her tail over and over until a flash of lightning struck nearby with a loud crack and the lights in the house went dark. The Christmas music stopped, and the sound of the wind competed with the crackling fire.

"Do you know where the fuse box is?" Sam asked calmly.

"No." Her voice didn't sound calm at all. "Maybe in the garage?"

Neither of them used the tiny one-car garage. It was filled with old woodworking equipment and boxes that belonged to their landlord. As soon as Sam scooted back from the table, Cuppie was on full alert. The two of them disappeared into the dark and came back a few minutes later.

"Found it," he said. "But the power's not coming back on."

The storm had darkened the sky so much that most of the interior light was coming from the fireplace. "Do we have any candles?" Sam asked.

"I have a couple."

"The outside woodpile's gonna be wet, so as soon as we go through these logs, it might get cold."

"How long do you think we have?"

"Three hours of heat. Maybe less."

"The power will come on before then," Allie said. That's how it used to work in Nashville, anyway. The power always came back on within the hour.

A torrent of rain hit the roof like a tidal wave curled onto the house. Allie gasped and instinctively ducked like the roof was about to cave in.

"How much battery do you have on your phone?" Sam asked.

"Zero." Allie hated admitting it. "I don't have my phone here."

Sam didn't react. "We can use my car to charge my phone. I'll monitor the radar."

"For tornadoes?"

"For everything."

Cuppie was back by the fire. Allie picked up her unfinished plate of food and sat on the hearth near her. "Our stove is electric, isn't it?"

Sam nodded, taking a seat on the couch opposite her.

"So are our microwave, refrigerator, and freezer." She groaned.

"Yep."

"I don't even have my car here." The words came with a hefty burst of shame that she quickly worked to push aside. "But we have yours, so we could go somewhere if we had to."

He chuckled. "This is absolutely not a life-and-death situation."

"Right," Allie agreed.

But it was a spending-time-with-Sam situation. A bonding situation. And a *this cozy fireplace feels kind of romantic* situation.

Chapter Eleven

THE TWO LITTLE candles Allie found were barely enough to light the bathroom, but they would have to do. The power had been out for four hours, and the storm still blustered and blew, blocking out the sun with a thick bank of black clouds. Allie, Sam, and Buttercup sat by a fire that was now just hot coals and some quickly disappearing cardboard Sam found in the garage. Allie wrapped herself in the lacy comforter from her bed, and Cuppie snuggled up with her, choosing the warmest spot possible underneath her left arm. The radar app on Sam's phone showed a huge swath of yellow and red that meant a long day spent inside.

Allie was hungry for something other than the Oreo cookies from her personal cabinet and the beef jerky Sam shared. "I'm going to cook us something over the coals," she said, disturbing Cuppie by standing. "Here you go, Cuppie-girl." She covered the dog with her comforter.

The refrigerator held enough food to last them for several days, and she rifled through it as quickly as possible, hoping not to lose too much of the cold. She found carrots and chicken breasts. In the pantry there was vegetable stock and an onion. It wasn't ideal, but with seasonings and maybe some teeny broken-up capellini noodles, she could make a decent soup. She chopped up the chicken and vegetables, added some olive oil, and scraped them into the base of her cast iron Dutch oven. Sam evened out the coals, and she set the pot on top, mixing occasionally. Chicken always tasted better when it was browned first, and it, along with the carrots and onion, browned quickly on the heat. She added the vegetable stock and waited.

Cuppie was very interested in what Allie was doing, her muzzle as close to the boiling soup as possible. Carrots took a long time to soften, and Allie hoped the coals would last. She and Sam took turns blowing on them, trying to extend the orange glow as long as possible. At one point, they blew at the same time, their faces closer than they'd ever been before. Allie laughed nervously. He wore a black winter coat and an army green knit hat, and she could feel the heat emanating from him more than from the fire. Her little sweatshirt wasn't cutting it. She pulled her comforter from the couch and wrapped it around her, then sat back on the hearth next to Sam. They were losing the fire, but at least they would have hot soup, even if the carrots were crunchy.

He caught her eye and smiled. She smiled back, momentarily forgetting that she didn't want to like him. He'd talked about chicks coming over. But really, it had been one silly comment that he'd probably meant as a joke. She hadn't so much as heard him talking to a girl on the phone, and there certainly hadn't been any at their house. She watched him from the corner of her eye as he prodded the fire. She had to admit that his broad shoulders, the shadow of a light beard, and his confident way of doing everything were attractive qualities.

There were some people who made you feel alone in their presence, like anything you cared about was of absolutely no concern to them. But Sam felt like a partner, like someone who was all in, and she knew for sure that if anything happened to her, he would do everything in his power to help. He would carry her with one arm, just like he did for Tulip.

Rain blew sideways onto the windows of the house, and the noise rattled Allie as much as the shutters. "It's crazy how fast these storms blow in," she said, trying to keep her voice steady. "It was so nice just yesterday."

Sam nodded in agreement.

"Maybe we should move away from the window."

Instead of ignoring her concern, Sam got up and checked every window at the back of the house. "They seem fairly solid, but I'll close the curtains just in case."

A closed curtain was better than nothing. And Sam taking her seriously was definitely more than nothing. She thanked him, but gratitude wasn't the only thing she was feeling. Looking at him gave her goose bumps. The room got progressively darker, and the dying fire popped, landing a piece of burning ember on Allie's blanket. Sam immediately flicked it off with his bare hand.

Safe. Cared for. She was feeling things she hadn't felt in years. Her lip quivered.

"Are you okay?" he asked, taking his seat on the hearth beside her. "Did the spark burn you?"

She shook her head, trying to hide the fact that tears were about to spill over. He swiped all over the comforter with his hand, then he did the same to her hair, gently brushing his hand over it, searching for anything that might be alight. She sucked in her breath and was afraid to let it out. He would be able to hear the nervous staccato of her exhale.

"You're trembling," he said, his hands on the blanket covering her upper arms. "Come here." He pulled her into his chest and held her, his right arm applying more force than his left. "You don't have to be scared," he whispered.

It wasn't the storm that made her emotional. It was the Christmas tree and the fire and the soup and the way she felt safe in that tiny house with him. She allowed herself to sink into his body, the threat of tears gone, but the threat of developing feelings for him stronger than ever. She wanted to hate him. A girl couldn't fall in love with her roommate. That would be unseemly, and it would put them both in a vulnerable position. What would happen if someone got their heart broken? They would still have to see that person every day. That would be crazy. She would be stupid to allow any feelings aside from the possibility of friendship.

She felt his chest rise and fall under her cheek, his heartbeat strong and sure. He was like their house in the storm, solid and quietly strong enough to keep them both protected from the onslaught.

"I'll serve us up some soup," she said, pulling away.

"I'll get the soup," he said, but he didn't move to leave.

"Thank you." She scooted away from him and cuddled up with her blanket. "My comforter smells like smoke. I'm gonna have to wash it."

He paused like he had something to say but wasn't sure if he should. "Hey, Allie?"

She had just pulled the blanket up over her head so only her face was showing. She turned to face him, fairly certain she looked like a Russian nesting doll.

"You're beautiful."

There was no expectation on his face, but his eyes crinkled in the corners as they boldly looked straight into hers. She immediately looked away. "I need to—" She stood and bunched the blanket in her arms. She needed to leave. She should go. A line had just been crossed, and that was dangerous.

No more bad choices, she told herself. *But what difference would one more make?* Dammit, she was going to let whatever happened happen today. She threw the blanket to the floor and sat back down beside him. "You think I'm beautiful?"

He nodded. "I do."

The truth was, he was one of the most attractive men

she'd ever seen, but she couldn't bring herself to tell him that. It would be giving up some of her power. Just because he'd said it to her didn't mean she had to say it back. She wasn't ready to be vulnerable. She might never be ready. Opening her heart to someone meant she could lose them. He was so bold in the way he kept his eyes on her. And he had that half grin that he always seemed to have around her. His nearness was still imprinted on her—his steady heartbeat and strong, even breaths.

Would his lips be soft? Or would they be firm and bold? Kissing him could be nothing. She'd had meaningless kisses before. Or kissing him could be something. It could change everything. But she didn't have to decide what it meant just then. She could decide later if she wanted more kisses or if they should just be friends. A kiss didn't mean a relationship. So, she should kiss him. She should absolutely kiss him. She bravely moved her face toward his.

"Don't mess with me." His voice was deep and pleading, making it clear that she had the upper hand. But he didn't move. He was just inches away. She felt his warmth and parted her lips slightly, then closed her eyes.

It was the slightest brush of skin at first, the gentlest sigh of a kiss. Then a pause to ensure it wasn't a mistake. His lips touched hers again with both pressure and restraint, both soft and firm, not one or the other. He was careful, respectful, but there was a passion underneath—one that made her dizzy. Each kiss built with intensity, his breath short and choppy against her lips. She abruptly turned her head away.

"Allie—" Sam began.

"Don't tell anyone about this. This didn't happen." Cuppie barked as Allie walked as fast as she could from the room. She locked the door to the bathroom where one remaining candle gave off barely enough light to see. What had she done? Yesterday she'd tried to kiss her coworker and today she'd kissed her roommate. The water was as cold as possible as she splashed it on her face over and over again. Then she brushed her teeth, even though it felt like she was scrubbing Sam away. She didn't want to scrub Sam away. She wanted to keep Sam close. And that was exactly why she needed to brush harder.

She closed the toilet seat and sat with her head in her hands. How was she supposed to walk back out there? She looked around at the man stuff in the bathroom—a bottle of three-in-one shampoo, conditioner, and body soap, his thin navy blue towel next to her fluffy white one, a black toothbrush, plug-in razor, and deodorant. She already knew what his soap and his deodorant smelled like. Now she knew what he felt like too. He felt good. Too good. Exciting. She had no intention of leaving that bathroom, until she remembered—soup. Eating the soup would give them something to do. Then she wouldn't go near him again. His words rang in her ears: *Don't mess with me.* She wasn't messing with him. She was messing with herself. He had family in Montana. He had a dog. She had nothing. She was the one whose heart was on the line.

She grabbed her winter coat from her bedroom closet and pulled on her leather gloves before heading out to face the consequences of her actions. She hadn't noticed that the storm had briefly quieted, and she hadn't heard the doorbell ring. But when she walked back into the main living area of the house, she found Sam talking with Tulip and Jessa.

Chapter Twelve

"THEY BROUGHT COOKIES!" Sam said, pulling Tulip into his side. "Tulip made 'em."

"Chocolate chip." She snuggled happily into the spot that appeared to be quickly becoming her most treasured place.

Allie tried to pull herself together and act normal. She had never been a fan of unannounced visits, and it felt like her neighbors were experts in it. "My favorite."

"I'm so happy y'all are okay. Joey said he's been trying to reach you, Allie, but you haven't responded at all."

"I left my phone at work."

"Oh." Jessa's sweet smile was suddenly back. "Well, then use my phone. That man is beside himself with worry."

The last thing Allie wanted to do was call Joey when just moments before she'd been locked in a passionate kiss with Sam. "It's okay. I'll talk to him on Monday."

Jessa shook her head. "The man will die of worry before then." She laughed. "You might as well be committing a murder."

Allie was confused. Why would Joey even care? Was he

that desperate for her to apologize to him?

She leaned in and whispered, "He said y'all almost had a little thing."

From the look on Sam's face, he'd heard every word.

"What we had was too much wine. Well, I did, anyway." The heat of embarrassment creeping up her face was painfully familiar. "Can you just tell him that you saw me and that I am truly sorry? I'll apologize again when I see him at work."

Jessa squinted at her.

"Oh, and can I hitch a ride in on Monday?" Allie added, desperate to change the subject. "My car's there too."

Jessa frowned at her. "I'm trying to tell you that Joey likes you, ya dumbhead."

Dumbhead?

"And of course you can have a ride."

Allie's heart dropped to her stomach as she whispered to Sam, "Excuse us." She motioned for Jessa to follow her into her bedroom, then shut the door, grateful for the tiny bit of diffused light coming in from the window. "What do you mean, he likes me?"

"Listen, he wouldn't have told me except for that he was worried because you haven't been responding to your texts or calls. He's afraid he messed up."

"He didn't mess up—I did." And now, thanks to Jessa's visit, Sam probably thought she was the hook-up queen of Goose Island. "I feel like I just ran into a wall," Allie said, sitting on the bed. "My head hurts."

"Oh, honey." Jessa patted her on the shoulder. "Sometimes walls are put there for us to lean on."

It was such a compassionate thing to say, so spot-on, that combined with all of the other crazy emotions she'd experienced in the past twenty-four hours, Allie was afraid she'd either burst into tears or laugh like a maniac. "I can't talk to Joey right now, Jessa. I just can't."

Jessa must have some of whatever it was that Dottie possessed, because she was really good at sussing out situations quickly. "I'll handle it, Allie. Don't worry."

Allie squeezed the hand on her shoulder. She might be making a friend on the island after all.

"You know," Jessa said, "my little sister has a crush on your roommate."

"I think even the dog knows that." Allie laughed, grateful for the change of subject. And in that moment she knew—she was developing a crush on Sam too. "Let's go back out before they wonder about us." The hallway was so narrow, the girls walked shoulder to shoulder. "So, do y'all have power?" Allie asked, thinking about the plate of warm cookies and the fact that she was starving.

"Naw, but the stove is gas, so Mama and Tootie have been at it, baking up everything in the pantry. Then Uncle Fred and Whiskey came over, and I tell you what, I was glad that Toots demanded to come here in the rain because between the dog terrorizing Mama's cats and Fred bringing the tequila, it's louder than an SEC game over there."

Dottie and Fred drinking tequila? The thought of Santa and the psychic drunker than skunks made Allie laugh. "Y'all are welcome to stay for some chicken soup," she said. "We just cooked it over the coals."

"Hey, Toots!" Jessa said. "These campers just invited us to stay for soup."

Tulip was sitting as close as possible to Sam on the couch. She gave a satisfied little nod before snuggling even closer. Sam looked both honored and mildly uncomfortable.

"We'd love to," Jessa said.

No sooner had they sat at the table with their steaming bowls than the front door sounded like it was under attack by a monster-sized woodpecker. The knocks were loud and fast. Cuppie was at the door and barking before Sam had a chance to get up from the table.

"It's got to be Mama," Jessa said with a sigh.

"Is she gonna make us come home?" Tulip looked distressed.

As soon as Sam twisted open the lock, the door opened and Dottie and Fred entered like stampeding elephants.

"There y'all are!" Dottie declared, blowing past Sam to the kitchen with Cuppie on her heels. "It's Saturday night, and I am not spending it alone with my brother." A loud roll of thunder emphasized her words.

Fred ambled in behind her, taking his time. The minute he stepped into the family room, he noticed Sam's little red stocking. "Where's yours?" he asked Allie.

Allie blew it off with a shrug, so Sam clarified for her. "She's taking a little break from Christmas traditions."

Fred chewed on his ever-present toothpick as he looked around the room. "You put up that tree?" he asked Sam.

"Yessir."

"Well done, soldier."

It was clear from Sam's face that *soldier* was meaningful to him. It was a term of respect.

"Would y'all like some soup?" Allie offered.

"Hell yeah." Dottie was already seated at the table, and Fred pulled up the last chair next to her.

Tulip was almost done slurping her soup by the time Allie served Dottie and Fred. "Uncle Fred," Tulip said, "did you know that if you say the word *colorful*, it looks like you're saying I love you?"

"*Olive juice* works for that too," Fred said, blowing on the steaming broth.

Tulip made a show of turning to Sam and mouthing, "Olive juice."

"Colorful," Sam mouthed back as Tulip giggled.

"How ya feelin', darlin'?" Dottie asked Allie.

"Like an idiot."

"I don't see an idiot." Dottie stared at Allie like she could see straight through her. "But you're giving too much power to negative thoughts. You know, a rising tide lifts all the goats." She reached across the table to touch Allie's hand. "Work on your thoughts, lift them up, and you can still get what you want." The whole table was listening. "And what might that be, the thing that you want?"

"Alright, now, Dot. Let the girl be," Fred interjected with a piece of noodle stuck in his beard.

"I don't know." Allie shrugged. "My dad back?"

Dottie shook her head. "Dig deeper."

"Control over my life?"

"And…"

"A future that doesn't include me being alone?" She felt the weight of Sam's eyes heavy on her face. "Or maybe I just need to accept that my life will never be happy again."

"No maybes," Dottie said. "Maybes ain't of no use at all."

That was not the response Allie expected, and frankly, she was tired of being on display while she tried to come up with an answer. "You know what? After my dad died, not only did my mother move away from my childhood home, but she threw away everything. I mean, *everything*. My trophies, my high school yearbooks, even the teddy bear she sewed for me from scraps when I was a baby. So, I'll ask you. How would that make you feel? Secure? Happy? Like you have a strong family to fall back on? Anyway, she has a boyfriend now, so she doesn't need me."

Dottie just smiled like she was freaking Zen Buddha and had all of the answers. "So, what you want is…"

"To be left alone." Allie scooted out her chair and stood. "I don't mean to be rude. Please excuse me." She walked out of the room having never taken even one bite of soup.

"Dang it, Dot. As soon as you get to drinkin' you start pecking away at people," she heard Fred say.

And then "I'll talk to her" from Jessa before Allie shut and locked her bedroom door.

Thankfully, someone must have decided to give her some time. No one came knocking. But now, she was stuck in her room ashamed of behaving like a spoiled child, and her only warm blanket was in the family room in the shape of a ball and covered with dog fur and ash. Her bed had a top sheet, but there was nothing else to cuddle up in. It was like a metaphor for her life. She was alone and freezing.

Through the thin walls, she heard Tulip start to sing a Christmas carol. She strained to listen. It was "We Wish You a Merry Christmas," but Tulip must've only known the chorus, because she sang that portion three times in a row. Then the whole group sang "Jingle Bells," and Allie covered her head with her pillow.

But it was when Sam started in with an old Elvis Christmas classic that Allie's stomach turned sour. Panic attacks always happened that way. First with a déjà vu, and in this case, it was her father doing his yearly Elvis impression. "Blue Christmas" was his signature Christmas song and the only one within his very limited vocal range. It was one of her favorite parts about Christmas—her dad all smiles and silly Elvis moves.

Nausea always hit next with a panic attack, then her arms

went numb, her heart raced, her brain went foggy, and darkness filled her soul with a powerful dread that something horrible was about to happen. Something she couldn't wrap her mind around, no matter how hard she tried. With each attack, she feared she might not survive. But she'd had enough of them now to know that they wouldn't kill her. The attack would pass, and she'd be herself again. The trick was to let it happen, ride it out, and try not to think too much until the world righted itself again.

Chapter Thirteen

DOTTIE PUSHED THE sweat-soaked hair from Allie's face. She was back from the edge of oblivion thanks to Cuppie, who must've sensed something because she beat her nose against the door until Sam ran over to see why. It was Sam who picked the lock to Allie's bedroom door and Dottie who ran in to tend to what must've looked like a corpse in the middle of the bed. Allie had gone into a cold sweat, and she knew from previous experiences that her lips lost color and her eyes went glassy. She couldn't understand the first few things Dottie said—they sounded like they were softly echoing in a cave—but she felt her touch and was grateful. As she pulled out of the attack, words began to make sense again, and she realized that Sam was holding on to her wrist, taking her pulse.

"I'm okay," she whispered. "It's just a panic attack."

"Just?" he said, sitting on the bed beside her. "How often do you get them?"

"Not often."

"Too much of the unseen is getting in." Dottie seemed concerned. "Some of it's okay; you grow when you're uncomfortable. But this is too much."

"Grow?" Allie squeaked. "I should be really tall by now." She could joke because it was over, even though she still felt weak and heavy.

"Are you sure you're okay?" Sam asked.

"I'm sure." With some help from Dottie, she was able to sit up. There, in her doorway, were Jessa and Tulip, both looking stricken. "Hey," Allie said. "Sorry to scare you. I promise I'm fine."

"Uncle Fred went to get y'all more wood from Mama's house," Tulip said. "It's too cold in here. Someone could get sick."

"Should we stay or let y'all be?" Jessa asked. "We've got just about everything anyone could want back at the house if y'all need anything. Anything at all."

"What time is it?" Allie asked Sam.

"Just a hair past six," Dottie answered.

"A little rest sounds good."

Dottie clapped her hands together. "Girls, make Allie a bed on the couch, and when Fred gets back we'll stoke the fire. We won't leave until we get y'all situated."

"You can use the blankets from my bed," Sam said. He must've noticed Allie's lone sheet. "You got a favorite pillow?" he asked her.

Just as she nodded and pointed to the squishy one behind her head, they heard the front door open. It sounded like Fred back with firewood.

Sam leaned toward Allie. "Put your arms around my neck," he said, sliding his good arm underneath her legs. He lifted her easily. "You got the pillow, Dot?"

"Got it."

By the time they got to the couch, Sam's blankets were neatly spread out. He placed her on top of them and folded them over her as Dottie placed the pillow behind her head. Cuppie jumped onto the couch and snuggled next to Allie before anyone could stop her. Sam said her name in a stern tone, but Allie stopped him. She wanted the dog there.

"Your soup's cold," Jessa said, "but I put it in a mug to make it easy to drink."

"Thank you," Allie said, meaning it. "All of you. Thank you so much."

Fred stopped stacking firewood long enough to turn and say, "This is what neighbors do."

"Yeah, we piss you off and then we make it up to you." Dottie laughed.

Fred made a few more trips for extra firewood, then, as promised, the whole crew disappeared. They left behind the snapping sparkle of a warm fire, sweet chocolatey cookies, and silence. Sam lifted Allie's legs and sat on the couch beneath them. "What a day," he said.

"Oh my God. You're not kidding."

"You can call me Sam."

It wasn't that funny. It was actually kind of obnoxious, but something about Sam's unexpected little joke tickled

Allie. It started in her belly, then quickly turned into a full-fledged laughing fit. Once he joined in, she couldn't stop. Cuppie looked at them like they'd lost their minds.

"My stomach muscles hurt," she said, finally beginning to calm. "Don't ever do that again."

"Right back at you. Don't ever scare me like that again."

"Well, if we're keeping score, you scared me first with your whole nightmare thing." She saw him deflate with her words, but it still felt right to bring it up. "I'm panicking over invisible things and you're shooting at them." She hadn't realized the similarities until the words came out of her mouth.

He nodded as he took it in. "What a pair we make."

"A pair of messes."

"No." His eyes stayed firmly on hers as he shook his head. "We don't have to be perfectly healed in order to be accepted and cared for. We can still be works in progress."

She took some time to think about what he'd just said. "That is healing, isn't it? Letting what might be the worst version of yourself be loved? We don't have to be perfect. We feel things. And that's good."

"And we live in a world where people shoot each other and freeze in the middle of winter storms and get lost on wild islands while looking for sharks' teeth."

"And we also live in a world where neighbors bring cookies and build fires and make beds on a couch," she said.

"And dogs sense things we can't and people get drunk,

and"—his eyes twinkled over his sly smile—"and roommates kiss."

Allie grabbed the pillow from behind her head and covered her face. "That's a secret."

"Don't you dare regret it," he said, teasing in his voice. "You like me, you know you do."

She shook her head underneath the pillow, which smothered her words. "No, I don't."

"What's that you're saying? I can't hear you. You think I'm handsome?"

She shook her head vigorously.

"Oh, I get it. You're in love with me."

She laughed underneath the pillow.

He chuckled. "I might be willing to kiss you again. I mean, if you're gonna force me."

She kicked her legs, and he held them down, so she pulled off the pillow and whacked him on the head with it. "That's all you're gonna get," she said.

Now Sam had a hold of the pillow, which was quickly thrown on the floor. Cuppie jumped off the couch when the ruckus began, so Allie had room to pull up her legs and sit facing him. "You're the one who's in love with me," she said, one-upping him at his own game.

"That's a mighty big word to throw around like that."

"You started it!" The man was exasperating.

He scooted closer, and she knew exactly what he was doing. It was written all over his suddenly serious face. His hand slid up to her cheek as he went to close the gap between their lips. Allie leaned over to the coffee table and picked up her mug of soup. "I'm hungry," she said, taking a cold sip.

He backed off immediately, and she felt his disappointment. It took him a while to recover before he said, "I'm not mad, okay. It's all cool either way. I just need to know. Do you like that other guy?"

So, he'd definitely heard what Jessa said about Joey. Allie put the soup back on the table. "I thought maybe I liked him because he reminded me of someone I used to know."

"And now?"

She shrugged. There was no use pretending. The fact was, she didn't know how she felt about Joey, aside from embarrassed. "I guess I'll have to see how things go at work on Monday."

Sam nodded slowly. "So, I'm the casserole in the warming drawer."

"What?"

"My mother used to put casseroles in the warming drawer underneath the oven. She kept them warm until it was time to serve 'em up. Looks to me like you're trying to keep me warm until you decide."

"What am I supposed to do? I barely know either of you. I need some time to figure things out." Men were all about instant gratification, all the time. See, want, take—that's how they operated. "Would you rather me stick you in the freezer?"

"Maybe I need to stick myself in the freezer." He scooted over, picked up the pillow, and handed it to her. Then he patted the couch for Cuppie to come sit between them. Allie lay down, her feet underneath the dog's belly with Sam on the far end of the couch. The ambient noises were suddenly back—the crackling fire, the whooshing wind, the soft breathing of the dog.

Soon, every living thing on the couch was sound asleep.

Chapter Fourteen

SUNDAY MORNING ROSE sunny and warm, sending streams of light onto the slumbering pile on the couch. The fire was spent, and the air around them cool—the only source of heat seemed to be the dog, who took up more space on the couch than either human.

"Still no power?" Allie asked when she realized Sam's eyes were open.

"I'll try the breaker," he said.

The circuit breaker was in the tiny garage, pitch black and a veritable conservancy for multiple species of spiders. "Want me to come with you?" she asked.

"Naw, I got it. Gonna have to charge my phone in the Jeep after using the flashlight app, though."

"Maybe we'll get lucky with the power," she said, stretching her legs out straight before standing. She padded behind him to the small door at the end of the hallway. A puff of dust fell from the top of the door when he opened it, adding a layer of grayish white to the short sleep-pressed swoops of his hair. He shook like a dog and brushed it off before heading down three steps into the concrete room.

She watched him disappear as Cuppie stayed beside her. A smile spread across Allie's face. "Watch this, Cup," she whispered. Carefully, toe-heel, toe-heel, she tiptoed down the steps. She was well out of the way of his flashlight as she ducked behind a rickety highboy dresser stored with other old furniture off to the left. She heard the squeak of the fuse box door and tried to suppress her laughter. If the lights came on, she'd be caught. But if they didn't, she was about to scare the bejesus out of brave soldier Sam Clare. Giggles bubbled up, and she held her breath. From the top of the stairs, Buttercup howled. Her adults had gone crazy, and there were questions in her tone.

"Cut it out, Cup!" Sam called. "Give me a sec."

He was flipping switches back and forth, but so far, no light. Allie shook with anticipation. She was about to get him good. Bits and pieces of the room were visible from the wide angle flood beam of his light, and the effect was chilling. The worn antique furniture didn't help at all. She imagined a creepy old doll coming to life and saying horrifying things in a voice that sounded like a hiss.

She was supposed to be scaring Sam, but instead she was scaring herself.

"No luck," he yelled, closing the metal door of the box. Cuppie barked, but Allie remained silent, shivering, ready to pounce.

He was almost to the stairs, and it was all Allie could do not to laugh. Should she yell "Boo!" or should she scream?

He was almost to the highboy, and she was well-hidden from the light. Three, two—

She was about to spring when Sam turned off the flashlight. Now the only source of dim light was from the hallway. Cuppie howled again. Sam walked backward into the pitch black and with the deepest, creepiest voice she'd ever heard, said, "You can't hide from the garage monster." He took in a Hannibal Lecter breath and said, "I've been waiting for you."

Allie screamed and ran up the stairs as fast as she could with Sam on her heels. Cuppie barked and jumped maniacally as they both made it down the hall to the front door. She twisted the handle and ran outside, down the front steps, and to the passenger side of Sam's Jeep, where she finally bent over to catch her breath. Her fuzzy socks were muddy, and her eyes felt as round as his oversized all-weather tires as they took in the sight of him bent over laughing at her from the porch.

"Gotcha," he said, walking down the steps into the rain. He pulled her into a hug and held her tight, allowing the rain to flow over them both.

She couldn't be mad. She knew it. She was as stiff as a shotgun and wanted to punch him. But the tighter he held her, the more her body relaxed into him, her heart rate slowly returning to normal. She finally pulled away. "How'd you know I was there? I was so quiet!"

"You forget, I'm a trained warrior. Every sense is honed."

"Right." She wiped the wet hair from her eyes. "You're a ninja."

"Army Ranger."

"No, you're not. You said you were search-and-rescue." They walked back to the front door together. "Or you have a CrossFit membership, so now you think you're a Ranger."

"I'll show you my Ranger tab."

"And I'll show you my Academy Award." She walked past him, pulling off her socks before she stepped into the house. She acted like she didn't care at all, but the fact was, she liked that he knew she was hiding in there. He could probably protect her, or at least help her survive, if the bridge to the island washed out and a cyberattack stopped the flow of the gas pipelines so freighters couldn't reach them and the electricity never came back on and zombies attacked the island. She tapped her pinky finger three times on the corner of the entry table while passing by.

She'd just grabbed two dish towels from the kitchen when there was a *boom!* and the lights and furnace flicked on. "Power's back!" she yelled, thinking Sam was still on the porch. Maybe he really was a ninja, because she hadn't heard or sensed him standing directly behind her. A sharp spurt of adrenaline flooded her body for the second time in the past three minutes. "Stop that!" She pressed a dish towel into his chest, and he used it to dry his hair.

"Too bad," he said. "I kinda liked life without power."

"Then feel free to live in a tent in the backyard." She was

a little surprised at how mean she sounded.

"So, the lights come on and you go back to hating me?" He opened the door to the refrigerator to check that it was back up and running.

"Yes." It somehow felt good to snap at him. She felt powerful and in control.

"So, you hate me," he clarified, shutting the refrigerator door.

She almost said yes again, but it was too big of a lie. Why was she so hot and cold with him? Just a few seconds ago, she was warm and happy in his arms. "Of course not."

"Okay." He wiped down both of his arms. "You want to bite me with your words? Go ahead. Take a chunk."

Calling her out had the exact effect of making her no longer want to do it. "You make me crazy," she said, but she couldn't help but smile. She caught a flash of blond hair flit past the window by the front door. "I think Jessa's back." Cuppie was already at her post, sniffing the doorjamb. Sure enough, the doorbell rang.

"Hey, y'all," Jessa said. "Sorry to bother you again. I just need to tell Allie something real quick."

Allie stepped back outside and shut the door behind her.

"I have to give you a heads-up," Jessa said. "Joey said he's going to the winery to get your phone. He's gonna bring it to you."

"Joey's coming here?"

Jessa nodded. "And I didn't want you or Sam to be surprised."

"Thank you, Jessa." Allie's heart was racing. "I mean it. Thank you so much." Jessa turned to leave, and Allie called out one last question. "How much time do you think I have before he gets here?"

"Don't really know, but I'm sure the streets around here will slow him down. They've got to be flooded."

Allie hadn't even brushed her teeth since spending the night on the couch, and she was currently sopping wet. She ran forward to lightly hug Jessa goodbye before scurrying inside to hop in the shower, feeling like she'd just had three cups of espresso even though they hadn't had a thing to eat or drink all morning. The light came on in the bathroom just like it was supposed to. *Thank God.* She turned on the shower water and brushed her teeth at the sink while she waited for it to heat.

Joey was coming over. Joey, who looked like Mark. Joey, who wasn't Mark at all. Joey, whom she'd tried to kiss. Joey, who saw her so drunk that her eyes floated like inflatable swim rings in a whirlpool. Joey, who brought her coffee, smelled like old man cologne, and looked great in a pair of khakis. Joey, who would probably scream louder than her if startled in a dark garage. She spat toothpaste into the sink and rinsed it, then turned the faucet off and on three times. Then one more time because the number three wasn't right. Then, two more times because maybe it actually was.

She took off her layers of clothes and shivered before

stepping into the steamy water. How was she supposed to act when he showed up? How was she going to apologize? And most importantly, how was she going to keep Joey away from Sam?

Chapter Fifteen

IT WASN'T LIKE Allie had taken an extra-long shower. It only took an extra five minutes to shave her legs. But when she walked into the hallway, she distinctly heard two male voices talking in the kitchen. It was becoming normal to sprint to her room from the bathroom. Not only was she a soaked rat, but Sam and Joey were clearly having a full-on conversation about something. What did they have to talk about aside from the weather and her?

She pulled on her underthings as quickly as she could and rifled through her closet for a clean sweatshirt and yoga pants. They wouldn't mention personal things, right? Like making out on the couch? Men didn't talk about that stuff. *Oh, please, don't let them talk about that stuff.* The last thing she needed was for the only two men on her roster to band together and turn against her. Women may have made progress on the sexual freedom front, but in the South, there were still the girls you hooked up with and the girls you took home to Mama. She needed to hurry. She brushed her long wet hair, added a touch of blush, lip gloss, and mascara, and it was time to scurry into the kitchen and break up whatever happened to be going down.

They were standing by the Christmas tree. Sam was showing Joey an ornament Allie hadn't even noticed. He had several *special* ones interspersed with regular red plastic orbs. It was a photo of Buttercup in an army green tactical vest. "Training is all about positive reinforcement," Sam said. "But first I had to build a relationship with her." He looked directly at Allie when he said the last part.

"Hi, Joey," Allie said, walking up to them. "Looks like you met my roommate." It sounded strange to say "roommate." She should've called him by his name. *Roommate* felt diminishing. He was more than just a roommate. Just like Joey might be more than just a coworker.

"Hey," Joey said. "Sorry for the unannounced visit, but I wanted to bring you your phone. Jessa said you left it at work." He handed her the pink-cased phone with the dead black screen. "It's not charged." His voice quavered like he was nervous. "I didn't want you to think I was trying to open it or something." Next, he handed her the brown bucket bag he had in his other hand—her purse.

"Of course not," Allie said, happy to have her things back. "Thank you so much." She bent to scratch Cuppie on the head, caught up in the relief of having her phone back. Normally, she couldn't go half an hour without it or her anxiety would skyrocket. What if there was an emergency and she needed to dial 911? What if there was a weather alert? What if the country was under attack and she had no way of knowing?

"Is Buttercup a good swimmer?" Joey asked Sam. "Her paws are huge."

"Very," Sam said in his typical authoritative way. He didn't appear to be in competition with Joey at all. "She's fast. The wolf in her can swim forever."

At the sound of Sam's voice, Allie knew instantly why she'd been okay for an entire day without her phone. It was because Sam made her feel safe.

Joey seemed impressed. "Cool."

Allie felt addled, a little shaken, or as her mother would say, *a bubble off plumb*. She was hyperaware that she was the only female in the house, and both men were, in different ways, dangerous. She had to say something normal, and be part of the conversation.

"Did you lose power at your place?"

Joey shook his head. "Some parts of Charleston went out, but not at my place."

Allie didn't know that he lived in Charleston. She'd assumed he had a place on the island. "You're in Charleston?"

He nodded. "I rent an old kitchen house behind one of the historic mansions south of Broad."

"That's so cool!"

Joey seemed pleased with her reaction. "You busy? I can take you out there now, show it to you. We could grab dinner somewhere on Bay Street."

Automatically, she looked over to Sam. He made intense

eye contact but nothing else. His face was absolutely expressionless.

"My hair is wet." It was all she could think of to say. Joey was asking her on a date, and just one day ago she would have been giddy. Now, she felt only dread.

"I can wait." Joey moved to the couch and sat like he already had his answer.

That move seriously irked Allie. She hadn't said yes.

It took a second, but just in time, Sam spoke up like she was supposed to know what he was talking about. "Fred will probably understand. But we did make a promise to him."

She knew he was trying to help her, so she went along with it. "Right," she agreed. "I would feel bad about going back on my word."

Joey stood. "Oh, are y'all helping Fred today?"

Allie nodded. "Yeah, sorry. Maybe I can see Charleston another time." She didn't say *with you* on purpose. After her night with Sam, she couldn't imagine going to another man's home or having dinner with him at some fancy place on Bay Street. But the look on Joey's face was her penance for changing her mind. He seemed genuinely disappointed. Which was strange, because he hadn't seemed interested at all Friday night at the winery. She'd been wholly and obviously pursuing him, and he'd pushed her away.

"What does Fred need help with?" Joey asked.

Panic. Complete and utter panic.

"Christmas cookies," Sam said easily. "Allie's mama has a

secret family recipe she promised to share."

Allie nodded with a smile as she wondered how Sam knew that her mama had a secret family recipe for Christmas cookies. Of course, every Southern girl had a secret family recipe for something. The cookie part must have been a lucky guess.

It appeared as if Joey believed them. "Alright, y'all. I guess I'll head on out, then." Cuppie led the way to the front door like she wanted to help speed up the process. "See you at work tomorrow, Allie."

Allie said goodbye, then yelled another thank-you for bringing her purse and her phone. As soon as she shut the front door, she realized she hadn't apologized for her drunken flirtations. Oh, well, waiting until Monday probably wouldn't hurt. She plugged in her phone and set it on the table next to the couch. "Well," she said to Sam, "you said it, so now we have to do it."

"Calling Fred now," he said, putting his phone to his ear.

An hour later, Allie's hair was blow-dried and pulled up in a ponytail. Fred handed them both candy-cane-striped aprons, and Sam got busy chopping Hershey bars to mix with unsweetened chocolate chips. The secret part to Allie's mother's chocolate pinwheel cookies was the mixture of the sweet and unsweet chocolates, plus the tiniest pinch of salt. The rest was like most cookies—butter, flour, sugar, eggs, and vanilla. The pinwheel part came with two batches of dough, one plain white and one made brown by mixing it with the melted chocolate. They were rolled out, stuck together, rolled up, chilled, sliced, and finally, baked, resulting in a cookie that looked like a whirly pop.

Allie's eyes kept going to Sam's hands as he worked. They were thick with callouses—a working man's hands. She remembered them so vividly on her cheek, in her hair, on her lower back. Fred hovered around them in his navy blue jumpsuit, his toothpick getting shorter and shorter as he flipped it and chewed. Country music crooned loud from ceiling speakers and, according to Fred, not one person had come into the store that morning, but they should brace themselves because the after-church crowd was due to hit soon.

Something about the cookies made Allie feel nostalgic. As soon as she put two more trays in the oven, she pulled out her phone to text her mother. She'd been in such a hurry to get ready to drive over to Fred's gas station that she'd barely looked at all of the unopened texts since Friday. There were at least fifty from Jessa and Joey. And one from her mother.

She clicked on her mother's text first. *"I love you, sweet girl. I will miss you this Christmas."* Immediately, Allie's stomach hurt. The ball was always in Allie's court. Why was Allie the one who had to travel? If her mother really cared, she would make the effort. And if she really cared, she wouldn't have thrown out Allie's things. And if she really cared, she wouldn't have immediately replaced Allie's dad with some other man. And, if she really cared, she wouldn't send her daughter guilt-inducing texts. So, no. She would not be going there for Christmas.

Next, she clicked on Jessa's texts, which consisted of varying versions of *"Are you okay"* and *"Call me, please."*

Then she clicked on Joey's. The man had practically written a book. *"I don't blame you for ignoring me,"* read the most recent. *"But if you're still interested in dating me, there are things you need to know."*

Oh, no. Allie cringed. Dating him? Oh, no, no, no. What had she done? She made sure Sam wasn't looking over her shoulder before she read on, knowing intuitively that whatever was coming wasn't going to be good.

According to Joey, it was time for him to invest in a woman again. He'd been trying to get over the breakup with his ex-girlfriend for the past two months. Rachel had been smart, sensitive, and feminine, and apparently, these and other things about Allie had reminded him of her.

It was like getting slapped in the face by her own hand. The whole reason she'd been attracted to him was because he reminded her of Mark. Now, there he was saying that she reminded him of Rachel. But instead of pursuing her because of their similarities, he had immediately friend-zoned her. Which was exactly what she should have done with him.

His texts were filled with regret. He shouldn't have bought her coffee or asked her to lunch. He'd been trying to be a good coworker. But when he was doing all of that, he had no idea that she liked him in *that way*. And now he was rethinking everything. He found her attractive and would like to see where things led, as long as they agreed to keep their work lives professional. And, maybe by being with someone who reminded him of his ex, he would be able to deal directly with that past pain and let go faster. His wordy, stream-of-consciousness paragraphs went around and around. It was like he was trying to convince himself of something, but was desperately unsure. The twenty-odd paragraphs he sent were absolutely the least romantic things she'd ever read. As a matter of fact, his words made her feel dirty—like she'd been trying to convince a reluctant virgin to have sex.

The buzzer on Fred's commercial oven brought her back to the present. Sam slipped mitts on both hands and pulled the large trays from the oven. "These might be the prettiest cookies I've ever seen," he said.

Allie didn't realize how much she needed Sam's positivity in that moment—how much she needed his approval—until she realized that with each word he spoke, she felt better.

"Your mama must be a good cook. These look like a pastry chef made them." He pulled off the mitts and popped a steaming-hot corner of a cookie into his mouth. "Mmm. They do not disappoint. You should definitely keep this recipe a secret. You might be onto something here."

Fred was like a giant brought in by the smell. *Fee fi fo fum.* "Good Lord, Miss Allie. These are mighty pretty. And they smell better than gingerbread."

"Thanks," she said, no longer feeling off-kilter. "They smell like the Christmases of my childhood. Mama said these were the best plate fillers."

"I tell you what," Fred said with a mouth full of cookie, "the good people of Goose Island are gonna thank you. These might not last a day."

"You're supposed to let those cool first." She laughed.

They both shook their heads at her, Fred with crumbs in his beard.

"Y'all got plans for Christmas?" Fred asked.

Allie looked to Sam.

"My old commanding officer is going to stop by," Sam said.

Allie's brow furrowed. "And I'm going to the beach."

"You're not celebrating?" Fred asked.

"Not last year, and not this year either." For the first time, she added, "But I'll get back to it eventually."

"No presents?" Fred said. "No big meal? No family?"

She caught Sam watching her carefully as she spoke. "My dad died three years ago. Three years ago tomorrow, actually, and my mother reacted by going way over the top with the traditions. I just want to take it easy."

Fred nodded, his bulbous nose highlighted by his fluffy beard and bookended by his twinkling eyes. "I noticed you didn't have a stocking up."

"Pretty sure Santa is not planning to squeeze himself down my chimney and fill my sock with goodies." There was an exchange of some sort between Fred and Sam. It was just a glance, but Allie saw it. "Stop it, you two. I don't need anyone to fill my stocking or rescue me. It is my choice to make, and I choose to do something else."

"Yes, ma'am," Fred said with a mock salute. Sam copied him, his salute crisp and genuine.

After they'd cleaned up Fred's kitchen and placed the cooled cookies in the glass display, Sam led Allie to the car. "So, tomorrow is the day, huh?"

She knew immediately what he was talking about. "Yes, and when I get home from work, I will probably go straight to my room, so don't worry about me or anything. I'll just want to be alone."

"I'll bring you some dinner." He held the passenger door open for her.

"I won't want to eat it." She climbed in, and he shut the door and ran around.

"How do you know?" he asked as he buckled.

"Because just thinking about tomorrow makes me lose my appetite."

He was quiet as they pulled onto the road leading home. Then he suddenly broke the silence. "How'd he die?"

"Cancer."

"How long did he fight?"

"More than two years."

He nodded like he was deep in thought. "Have you heard of anticipatory grief?"

"No."

"Can I tell you?"

She nodded, noting how careful he was with her.

"Well, grief doesn't actually start on the day a person dies. It starts on the day you think there's a chance it might happen. You've actually been grieving your dad to some degree for five years."

Allie sat with that notion. "But it's worse when he's gone, and I can't even talk to him about it." Something burned in her stomach and chest. She wasn't mad at Sam. But the burning felt like anger and self-pity and sadness and a desperate need for something she couldn't have. "I'll never, ever see him again. Do you know how final that is? My eyes miss his face. My ears miss the sound of his voice. Have you ever reached desperately for the hope that you once had, and it's out of reach forever? There's nothing you can do. No one you can beg or bribe or trade. You can't wish or pray or negotiate your way out of it. It's the emptiest, darkest thing."

"I know," Sam said simply.

She turned to the window and wiped tears from her eyes. Sam reached out and took her hand, steering with his weak left arm. He held her small hand in his large one until they parked in front of their cottage. "Hey," he said before she opened her door. "If you change your mind, you're invited to spend Christmas with me. Right here at home. No need to buy presents, sing songs, or watch any Christmas movies. You can just be with me."

"But your commander is coming over."

"It'll be brief. I promise. It's just a quick visit."

"Thanks, but I don't think I can." She opened her car door and climbed out.

"What about giving up the pain for just one day? What about taking a break?" he asked from the other side of the car.

She thought about it for a moment. "I'm too mad. At God, at my mom, at myself. I guess you could say that I'm mad at everything and everybody."

"Well, folks," he joked, "it looks like we need ourselves a Christmas miracle." They walked up the steps, and he unlocked the front door while Cuppie barked on the other side.

"Now you sound like a Hallmark movie." She attempted to open the front door, but he held it closed.

"Hey," he said. "Come here." It was becoming a normal thing, the way he pulled her into his chest and wrapped his arms around her, resting his lips on the top of her head.

She began to pull away, but he held her tighter.

"It's going to be okay," he whispered.

Once again, the longer he held her, the more she relaxed. Even Cuppie must've sensed something good was happening on the other side of the door because she quieted. He was warm and solid, his heartbeat steady, and his T-shirt smelled like cookies. She melted into him, and without thinking first, raised her chin, needing his warmth, his strength, and the soft diversion of his lips on hers.

The door became a bulwark as they leaned into it, no worry for the strength of the hinges or latch, just an urgent need for connection. There was no trepidation, no thoughts of Joey, just a primal, pure, chemical attraction let loose once again. Every inch of her was on fire. She didn't care that they were on the front porch and someone could walk up at any point and see them kissing. Nothing mattered but this man whose hands had made her mother's Christmas cookies. The man who took her grief seriously and hugged her like he genuinely cared.

She pulled away to look at his face. He was flushed, his eyes glassy with desire, and he looked back at her in a way she'd never experienced before—like she was precious, like her kisses were special gifts, and her attention was all he wanted in the world. She started to question how he could like her so much so soon. He'd seen her at her worst. She'd been sassy and mean. Then she captured those negative thoughts and threw them away. *Cherophobia*. She would choose happiness, even if just for a moment. No thinking, just feeling. On her tiptoes, she kissed him again.

His lips were ready to receive her.

Chapter Sixteen

ALLIE WOKE UP on the couch again, nestled into the dark blue of Sam's warm comforter, smashed up against his side with her head on his chest and Cuppie curled at their feet. Light seeped through the glass of the large kitchen bay windows. She stayed where she was, knowing by the sun's soft gentleness that it was still early. Sam's breathing was peaceful, his body relaxed, his heartbeat untroubled. He'd been so tender last night. For a man of such toughness, he wasn't pushy at all. Actually, he was the opposite. Where other men might be handsy, he was considerate. It wasn't like he was practicing patience with her—it was more like he truly wanted whatever was best for her. No hurry. No regrets. He would wait until she was in love with him. Kissing and cuddling was enough. She intuitively knew it.

It was impossible to imagine being annoyed with Sam now. His extreme good looks were no longer intimidating, his strong presence no longer unwanted. Her feelings toward him had flipped like a coin. He was heads-up now, and she wanted him near, wished she could snuggle into his side all day long. But it was Monday. A workday. Her apologize-to-

Joey day. And the three-year anniversary of the worst day of her life—the day that her dad died.

As soon as she stirred, Sam opened his eyes. "G'morning," he said, kissing her tenderly above her right eyebrow. "Big day. How ya doing?"

"You remembered." She sat up as he did, using his shoulder for lift.

"I'll make us some coffee," he said.

"Thanks," she said. "I have to get ready for work."

"You in a cereal mood? Feeling pancakey? Eggy?"

"Pancakey." She leaned into him, groggy, her hair flat on one side. He immediately wrapped his arms around her. She thought back to his earlier question—*how ya doing?* She was doing astonishingly well. The waves of grief that she expected to overtake her were still out to sea. Calm and peaceful. "What are you doing today?" she asked.

"I'm on the schedule for noon. I guess I'll see what dispatch has in store for us. It's a busy time for ambulances."

They'd gotten up early, so she had plenty of time to get ready. She showered, curled her hair, and even added foundation, eye shadow, and blush to her usual lip gloss and mascara routine. By the time she was finished, Sam had a pile of pancakes being kept warm on a plate in the oven, with his ear to his phone. "Yes, ma'am. I recommend taking her in to see a doctor. If there are white stripes in the back of her throat, it may be strep, in which case she'll need an antibiotic."

"You know what I think it is?" Allie could plainly hear Dottie's gravelly voice on the other end of the phone. "Lovesickness."

Sam laughed.

"You know she's wantin' to come over so you can take a look."

"Send her on," Sam said.

Allie loved the sound of his deep chuckle.

Dottie yelled at Tulip. "He said to go on over!"

Tulip was standing in their kitchen before Allie had a chance to eat one bite of pancake. She didn't look sick at all, but she did look cute with her bowl haircut pulled up on either side with pink barrettes. She wore blue eyeshadow too.

"Aaahhh," Tulip said as Sam shined a flashlight and looked in her throat.

"It doesn't look like pharyngitis," he said. "The tissues aren't bright red."

"It's probably just allergies," she said with not one speck of embarrassment. "Don't tell Mama."

"You going to school today?" he asked.

"No, it's Christmas vacation."

"Want some pancakes?"

She nodded again, this time with a sly smile and a twinkle in her eye. Clearly, her plan had worked. She was getting to spend time with Sam. "How do you like 'em?" he asked. "Well-done or gooey?"

He'd asked Allie the same thing. The well-done pancakes

were in the oven, but the gooey ones were made to order. He'd made the batter extra-thick so they wouldn't cook all the way through. Since Allie had never tried a gooey pancake before, that's what she requested. It was like an underdone biscuit—perfect with loads of butter and a little something sweet. Tulip opted for the same.

"Look at me, teachin' you girls how to eat," Sam teased.

Allie ate every last bite of her breakfast and rinsed her plate and coffee cup. She considered kissing Sam goodbye but didn't want to ruin Tulip's teenaged swoonfest. "Bye," she said as she grabbed her sensible satchel bag and headed toward the front door. "Have a good day." She'd completely forgotten that her car wasn't out front and that she'd asked Jessa to take her to work. *Shoot.* She pulled out her phone and texted Jessa. *"Have you left yet? I forgot that my car's not here."*

There was no answer. "Hey, Tulip?" Allie yelled. "Do you know if your sister is still home? I forgot that I need a ride to work."

"I can take you," Sam offered.

"She was home when I left," Tulip answered, stuffing a syrupy bite of pancake into her mouth. "Call her."

"I just texted, but she hasn't answered." Allie checked the time. She'd padded her departure with an extra ten minutes. Lateness was not something she allowed herself. She was always early, painfully so sometimes. She felt the jittery physical overflow of anxiety and tapped her fingers on her thigh, beginning with her pinky finger. Four-three-two-one, one-two-three-four. *Text back, Jessa. Text back now.*

Finally, just as her headache began, a chime sounded. *"Almost there,"* Jessa texted.

Allie exhaled. She wasn't going to be late.

"You need a ride home, Tootie?" Sam asked. "It's cold outside."

"Can you take me to my friend's house?" She smiled widely. It was clear that Tulip knew how to get what she wanted. "And can we bring Cuppie?"

Would Tulip ask him to walk her inside too? Few things would set more high school tongues to wagging than bringing a tall, handsome man and a wolf to her friend's house. Knowing kids these days, there would certainly be photographic evidence of it too.

A car horn honked outside. "Okay, y'all," Allie said. "That's my ride!"

"Hey," Sam said, catching up to her with a long-legged stride. "Come here." He pulled her in for a hug. She had her purse in between them, so he gently took it from her, placing it on the console table by the door. Then he hugged her again. "It's going to be a good day," he said, speaking into her hair. "And if you need me, just text or call."

She nodded, grateful that he was such a generous hugger. When he finally released her, Allie's eyes went to Tulip, who had put her fork down and pushed her plate away in disgust. Allie almost apologized, but that would be silly. Instead, she went over and gave her a hug too. "My dad died three years ago today," she said. "Sometimes we just need a hug."

Tulip straightened up immediately. "I don't have a dad."

Allie was once again surprised at how casual Tulip was about her parentage. But that was Dottie, she supposed—the woman couldn't keep hold of a secret if it was strapped like a belt to her waist. Whatever was in her head just slipped out as easily as *ands* and *buts* and *you knows*.

Jessa, on the other hand, probably knew everybody's secrets and never said a word. She was like the human version of sunshine. The ride to work was filled with giggles and smiles. Allie barely had time to think about her dad's death in between Jessa's hilarious griping about being stuck with her mother, a gaggle of cats, and a starry-eyed little sister during the storm. It wasn't until they pulled into the gravel parking lot of the Saltwater Winery that the weight of the dreaded day slammed down.

Joey was already at his desk. When Allie walked in, he spun around and stood.

"I got you a coffee," he said. "And Fred was selling some fancy new cookies. Are these yours? They're pretty good." He handed her one of her own spiral cookies. "You're not allergic to gluten, right? Rachel was, so I didn't know."

"I'm not. Thank you," she said, noting that she'd been there less than one minute and he'd already mentioned his ex-girlfriend.

"Joey, I need to apologize to you for my behavior Friday

night. I'm so embarrassed. I shouldn't have had that much to drink."

Instead of letting go, he took the coffee and cookie from her and placed them on her desk. Then he held both of her hands in his like he was about to make a vow. "I forgive you." His voice was so saccharine and his eye contact so direct that it gave her the ick.

Forgive? She'd been drunk, not evil. "Thanks." She had planned to say more, planned to actually use the words *I'm sorry*, but not anymore. And what was that smell? He must've doused himself in cologne. Being stuck in their tiny shared office with him all day was going to be nauseating. She squeezed his hands sweetly before pulling hers from his grasp. Then she sat in her chair and spun away.

A few hours into her workday, an email from Duke came through announcing that the winery would be closing early and everyone outside of guest relations could have the rest of the day off. Several employees had already taken the week off, and the whole place would be closed until Friday, so a little extra free time was welcome.

Joey spun around. "Wanna go to lunch? I still owe you a trip to Charleston."

Allie had to think quickly. "I'm so sorry. I have some last-minute shopping I need to get done." As soon as it came out of her mouth, it felt true. It wasn't too late. What if Sam had a gift for her and she didn't have one for him? That wasn't celebrating Christmas, that was just avoiding a potentially embarrassing situation. Gifts could be given at any time for any reason.

Joey looked disappointed, but he pushed ahead. "Do you have plans for Christmas Eve?" he asked. "My family has a big traditional supper if you want to join us."

Join his family? On Christmas Eve? The truth was, she had absolutely no plans for Christmas Eve. "I was planning to just relax this year."

"Come on, Rach—" His eyes went wide. "Allie. You can't do that. That's depressing. You're coming with me."

She hated when people told her what to do. "No, really. I'm just going to hang out at home."

"Absolutely not," he said. "I'm not going to let you sit at home when my family is making more food than we can eat. I'll pick you up at noon."

She decided to agree now and cancel by text later. "Great. Thanks." She internally cringed. One drunken night was wreaking havoc on her life.

Chapter Seventeen

THE PART OF Allie that felt sad wanted to go back to her little cottage and curl up under the covers. The covers that were still dirty with the smell of fire and dog and needed to be washed. If she was honest, the sad part of her was strangely comforting. As long as she was sad, she was honoring her dad. Joy would be offensive, like she didn't love him enough. If he looked down on her from heaven, she needed to make sure he knew that she missed him, knew that her life was not the same without him, that she needed him, and that his life on Earth made a difference to his one and only daughter. Without him, she was flesh without bones, canvas without a frame, a little pile of fluff without shape to hold her up.

She drove toward Charleston, spinning with the same thoughts she'd had for exactly three years. But this time, she wasn't crying. It was like every time she allowed the grief in, every time she felt sorry for herself, the intense emotions lost some power, loosened their hold. Slowly, she was incorporating loss into her life, learning how to navigate her new normal. If she weren't careful, she might actually end up happy again.

With each overcast mile, each signpost passed, Allie felt stronger. She was driving out of the anger stage of grief and into acceptance. Finally. When she drove past a roadside stand selling seagrass baskets and floral bouquets, she turned around and went back. Hanging from the rafters of the old nailed-together wood and tin lean-to were Christmas stockings. She picked out a large one, forest green with white trim. It felt overly optimistic to choose a stocking big enough to hold full-sized candy bars, new underwear, makeup, and still have space for her mother's tradition of a stuffed animal sticking out of the top. She wasn't getting any of that, of course. But there was room for it. Then she bought one for Sam, and a third for Cuppie.

It was almost noon, and she wasn't yet starving, thanks to Sam's pancakes. If she stopped by the grocery store, she could switch things up and make a meal for him. She wondered if he'd ever had a decent charcuterie board—the kind with brie cheese, honey, salami, grapes, and olives stuffed with almonds. She had a good job now. She could afford it. The excited feeling of planning a surprise made her smile—and drive more than her allowed five miles over the speed limit. Yes, she would surprise Sam with hors d'oeuvres, a good bottle of wine, and some sort of fancy homemade dinner. The plan made her feel like her old self again.

Parking was rough along King Street. Last-minute shoppers had lost time during the storm and were frantic to make up for it now. Christmas spirit was low and annoyance was high. Some folks didn't even make way on the sidewalk, just plowed down the middle, forcing others to yield to them. Two hours and several long lines at checkouts later, she held three bags—one from a custom knife store where she bought a hand-forged cleaver for Sam, one from a boutique where she found a soft sweater in her mother's signature eye-matching Carolina blue, and one from an upscale kitchen store that sold beautiful sets of olive oil and balsamic vinegar. She bought one each for Jessa, Libby, Joey, and Duke. It didn't matter that people around her were stressed and showing it—Allie felt great. She knew her dad would approve. Yes, he'd died just days before his favorite holiday. But maybe the way to honor him was not to have Christmas alone but to celebrate it in a way that didn't revolve around her mother, and didn't revolve around their pain. The thought felt better than anger and sadness. Maybe there was joy to be found in the traditions again.

"Is this what you want for me, Dad?" she whispered into the chilly Charleston air. "I think I can feel you with me."

The grocery store was worse than the shops, but she made it out with a big bone for Cuppie and a Christmas Eve spread that was sure to make Sam smile. She bought enough so that his visiting friend could have some too.

Cuppie announced her arrival when Allie pulled into the driveway, and stood squarely in her way, demanding attention, when she opened the door. "Just a second, Cup. I have to get this stuff to the kitchen." The dog buried her nose in the plastic bag holding salami, cheese, and her Christmas bone the whole way to the kitchen.

"You need help?" Sam asked, already heading for the door.

"You're home! I thought you had work this afternoon."

"I was there a couple of hours, then got someone to cover for me. There's an active search-and-rescue operation up in the Summerville swamps, and they need me and Cuppie. We were just about to head out."

"Who's missing?"

"An elderly man with dementia."

"Oh, no." Her heart immediately went to the family. "And right before Christmas."

He seemed seriously concerned about the old man, just like a search-and-rescue volunteer should behave—like he cared. "Listen," he said as he reached into the trunk of her car and hung every last bag on his flexed right arm. "I was hoping to talk to you tonight about my guest tomorrow. It's your Christmas Eve, too, even if you're not celebrating."

"It's okay. I don't mind." She would surprise him tomorrow with her new Christmas attitude. That would be fun. No need to tell him now. "I bought enough groceries to feed us all."

He looked surprised. "You did? I was going to do that—"

"All done." She slammed the trunk for added emphasis. Those two words were extraordinarily pleasing to say.

"You seem to be doing really well, considering the day," he said as she opened the front door for him. "I've been thinking about you."

"I'm okay," she said, surprised by the peaceful sound of her voice. "Don't worry about me, just focus on the lost man who needs you." They had the kitchen counter filled with plastic bags. "I'll put this away. You rush on out there."

He seemed nervous or jittery. Maybe it was the adrenaline of getting called in. She'd never seen him like that before. Aside from that one horrible nightmare, he'd always been calm and steady. Now he was practically vibrating, his eyes darting around.

"Cuppie! Heel." The dog was immediately on task, glued to his side.

And then they were gone.

Allie took her time loading the fridge and transporting the gifts from the back seat of her car into her bedroom for wrapping. Should she have gotten something for Dottie and Tulip? What about Fred? She checked her pantry. She could always make something sweet for them. That's what neighbors did, especially when they were new. They weren't close enough friends for store-bought gifts, but a sweet treat would work nicely. Her mother had the perfect recipe for those times when you needed something fast. It involved unlikely ingredients, like fiber cereal, that Allie happened to have on hand.

She pulled on her apron and set out the ingredients. She

couldn't believe it, but she was actually in the mood for Christmas music. When Bing Crosby began singing about white Christmases, she retrieved the stockings from the brown paper bag and took down Sam's tiny one from the mantel. She dug up a white paint pen and wrote their names in block letters onto the fabric encircling the top. ALLIE, SAM, and BUTTERCUP. Then she hung them up.

Her hands were covered in chocolate when Elvis began crooning about having a blue Christmas. Her dad's song. The one that couldn't come on without him vamping up his deep baritone and wiggling his hips. It triggered a shock of grief and loneliness, and she prayed it wouldn't trigger another panic attack too. She didn't want the comfort of her sadness in that moment. She had plans. Happy ones.

"Dad," she said into the air above the kitchen sink as she washed her hands. "I miss you. I can still hear your voice so clearly." The last sentence sparked the tears. "It's like someone came into my life and robbed me of my most precious thing, of my most loved person. And even if we caught them and put them in prison, we still couldn't get you back. God!" She threw the drying towel into the sink. That old mix of emotions was always ready to pounce. "I hate this!" Her legs felt weak, so she went to the couch and sat. "Mama has this stupid new boyfriend and she threw out all of my stuff and you're not there to make things better and I'm living with this guy on an island and now I think I like him and I shouldn't want to celebrate Christmas. But I do."

She stared at Sam's Christmas tree, breathing heavily, until the lights blurred together. "I don't want to feel this way anymore. This anger keeps popping up. I need to get rid of it."

It was barely perceptible. It might not have actually happened, but it seemed like every light on the tree blinked off and on in unison. Just once. Just enough to agree with her.

By the time Sam got home, two large trays of chocolate candies were hardening on the counter. The fiber cereal gave them crunch, the honey-roasted peanuts gave them a sweet saltiness, the cut-up marshmallows added a satisfying softness, and the mix of semisweet and milk chocolate was the perfect binder and complement. All of that without turning on the oven. But she did turn on the oven, because now she was in a baking mood. She made snowballs with so much butter that the powdered sugar on top turned into a sort of icing. They looked great on the plate for the Boones, but the assortment still needed one more thing. Maybe a bar of some sort—a dense brown-sugary oatmeal bar. She stood sprinkling sea salt over the hot bars when Sam walked in. He looked exhausted.

"Did you find him?"

He nodded sadly. Cuppie didn't even say hello to her. Normally, if Allie was in the kitchen, Cuppie was at her feet, hoping she'd drop something. Instead, the dog went straight to her fluffy round bed by the couch and curled up.

"Are you guys okay?"

"We will be," Sam said. "We've been through this before."

The air around them felt heavy. Allie knew the moment they walked in that the person they'd found hadn't been alive. "How'd he die?"

"It was a drowning." He plopped onto the couch with his arm over the side, petting Cuppie on the head.

"Cuppie's been through this before?"

"Cuppie and I found one of our best friends—" He didn't finish the sentence, but Allie knew. "He stepped on a device."

She sat beside him. "Do you want to talk about it?"

"Would you think less of me if I said I have a therapist?"

"No, I would think more of you." She put her hand on his knee.

There was something in his eyes that looked like relief. "I don't admit that to many people."

"Well, I'm your roommate. You can tell me anything. I'll be here for you whether you want me or not."

"My ride-or-die roomie."

"Roger that, soldier. Ride or die." She thought about saluting, but that was taking it too far.

He put his hand on top of hers. "Maybe I'll cancel my Christmas plans. It's hard to celebrate when there's so much to be sad about. We can both sit this one out."

"No," she said. "No, I was completely wrong about Christmas. We need to honor our loved ones. Not change things because of them. What was your friend's name?"

"Grayson Carter. But we called him Ghost." Redness appeared on his neck and flushed up to his face.

"And what was the man's name from today?"

"Robert Flack."

"I'll be right back." She ran outside to the woodpile where she'd seen half of an old flat piece of fencing. She brushed off the dirt and took it inside. "This will be our memory board." With the same paint pen she'd used for the stockings, she wrote MERRY CHRISTMAS on the top of the board, then began a list of names underneath beginning with PAUL WESTLEY, then GRAYSON CARTER (GHOST), and ROBERT FLACK.

"I have more names for that list," he said softly, his eyes bright with something that felt like surprise and appreciation.

"We have plenty of room."

Chapter Eighteen

SAM SUDDENLY NOTICED what was going on around him. The holiday music, the kitchen full of cookies. He sat up quickly. "You've been baking?"

"I have oatmeal bars fresh from the oven if you want a warm one."

That was all it took for him to jump to his feet. The sudden movement startled Cuppie. "Do we have milk?" he asked, surveying the counter filled with trays of sweets.

"Yes, we have milk."

"And I thought I couldn't love you more," he said. As soon as the words escaped, his eyes went momentarily wide. But he didn't take it back.

Allie pretended like she hadn't heard him. "I'll get you a glass."

"God, these smell good," he said.

"You can call me Allie." It took a second for the joke to register with Sam, but once it did, he couldn't hold back. She'd never seen him laugh so hard. Cuppie jumped up to check out what was happening. "I used his joke against him," she told the dog. "He thinks his jokes are the funniest." She gave Cuppie a treat and prepared a plate of cookies for Sam. Once the bellies of both of her human and her furry roommate were full, she turned on the television and looked for a Christmas movie.

Sam's phone rang.

"Sam Clare," he answered.

Allie could tell the voice on the other end of the line was male, but she couldn't make out the words.

"Yes, sir. Of course, sir. I look forward to it. See you tomorrow."

Sam was instantly back to looking stressed. "That was my old commanding officer. I meant to tell you earlier—he's bringing a guest." His phone rang again. "Hold up, Allie. Just a sec." He answered in the same way he had the minute before. This time when he hung up, he was pale. "Is it a full moon?" he asked. "There's another one. A missing teenager. I have to go." Cuppie seemed to know by the shift in Sam's demeanor that she was going back on duty. She was up and at his side without him asking.

"Do you want me to fix you a bottle of water? A sandwich? Do you know when you'll be back?"

"Naw, but thanks. I've got what I need. I just need to get there. They think the boy might be out near the beach."

"The beach? In the middle of winter?"

He shrugged and nodded.

"It's so cold, especially near the water. Make sure you wear a warm jacket."

He smiled at her. "Come on, Cup. Let's go find a kid."

And just like that, they were gone again, as was any desire she previously had to watch a Christmas movie. Maybe she'd just clean the kitchen and go to bed.

The house was strangely still when the sun rose the next morning. Allie's gifts were neatly wrapped and piled in the corner of her room, the heater softly hummed warm air through the ceiling vent, and her cozy comforter smelled like laundry soap, but something was off. She'd never heard Sam and Cuppie come home. She told herself that she'd just slept through it, but her intuition knew. They weren't here.

Wrapping herself in her pink bathrobe, she went out into the hallway. Sure enough, the door to Sam's room was wide open, his bed neatly made, and there were no sounds of a dog breathing, the click-clack of nails, or the thump of a wagging tail against the furniture. The kitchen and family room were as cold and empty as his bedroom. There were no calls, no texts, just silence. It was not quite seven A.M. He had guests coming in that day, so surely he would be home before they arrived. She had no idea when that was supposed to be.

She texted him, *"Everything okay?"* then immediately searched online for information about a missing teenager. From what she could tell, the search was still ongoing. A photo attached to the story showed a boat scanning dark ocean water with bright lights. Were Sam and Cuppie on that boat? It seemed impossible to find someone that way.

She prayed it wasn't going to end in another tragic loss. If anyone could find that boy, it was Cuppie and Sam. Those two would never give up. They'd survived God only knew what while they were in the military, and they knew how to keep themselves and other people safe. That made her feel a little better.

It was Christmas Eve. She had prep work to do for dinner and plates of Christmas cookies to deliver. But first, she went for a quick run. Exactly five miles. Then she took her time showering and curled her hair before carefully applying her makeup. The decision to open her heart to Christmas felt so good that she hummed happy songs as she piled cookies onto paper plates and covered them in cling wrap. It was cold outside, but the sun was large and bright. Exactly as it should be. She piled logs into the fireplace, placed twisted-up pieces of junk mail beneath them, then lit the flames. The papers caught quickly and burst to life. She plugged in the lights to the Christmas tree, and placed the gifts she'd stashed in her room underneath it.

Unless Sam put something in his own stocking, it was liable to be empty in the morning, so she folded a piece of printer paper into quarters and took out her set of markers. After drawing a Christmas tree on the front, she wrote inside: THIS CARD CAN BE EXCHANGED FOR ONE PICNIC ON THE BEACH. She almost added KISSES INCLUDED. But instead, she wrote WINE INCLUDED. Then she stuffed it into the open top of his stocking with one corner sticking out above his name.

There was still no return text from Sam, but he was probably busy searching. She put on her winter coat and grabbed a plate of cookies for the female Boones. As always, several cats sat in the front windows of the short brick home. She wished she'd thought to buy cat treats.

"Well, absence really does make the cookies look better," Dottie said the minute she opened the door. "Are those treats for us?"

"Merry Christmas!" Allie said.

"Come in, come in." Dottie ushered her inside and closed the door. "It's colder than a witch's toe out there. Carolina Jessamine! Tulip! Allie's here!"

A cat rubbed up against Allie's leg as she stood in Dottie's warm kitchen, so she bent down to pet it.

"That there's Starvin' Marvin," Dottie said. "He pretends like he ain't had a bite to eat in days, but don't you believe him. He eats more than the rest of 'em." Dottie peeled back the plastic film and popped a chocolate candy into her mouth. "Oh, yeah. That's what I'm squawking about," she said with a mouth full of food. "These are good."

"Hey, Allie!" Jessa was the first to enter. "Merry Christmas!"

Tulip was right behind her. "Is Sam with you?"

"No, he and Buttercup are working."

Tulip was obviously disappointed. She grabbed a cookie from the plate and headed back to her room.

"Tulip Boone." Dottie raised her voice. "Get back here this instant and say thank you to Allie. And Merry Christmas."

Tulip turned around and deadpanned, "Thank you and Merry Christmas."

"Merry Christmas," Allie said to her retreating back. The house was almost too warm and smelled of cats and fresh pine from the living Christmas tree in the corner of their overstuffed, over-knickknacked family room. There was not an inch of space that didn't have either a family photo, a living cat, or some sort of Christmas decoration.

Jessa pulled up a counter stool like she was settling in for conversation. "Whatcha up to today?"

"I'm gonna drop off cookies to Fred and then make some dinner. Sam's got people coming over, but I don't know what time."

"You're cooking for all of them?"

She shrugged. "Sam said they were just dropping by, but I want to make sure something's ready just in case."

"That right there is the mark of a good Southern girl," Dottie said. "Where'd you say you were raised?"

"Nashville."

"Yep. Your mama brought you up right."

People from other areas might not think that being called a good Southern girl was a compliment, but it felt good to Allie. She really had been raised well. As soon as she got home, she would give her mother a call and work out a time to give her the pretty sweater she'd found in Charleston. "What are y'all doing to celebrate?" Allie asked.

"Not cooking," Dottie said. "Which is why your cookies are most welcome."

"We do fast food at Christmas," Jessa said. "Like, whatever's open. We'll drive for miles and miles to pick it up. Last year we had Taco Bell on Christmas Day."

"I've got some holiday advice for you since ya got folks coming over," Dottie began. "Endurance is not hospitality. Got it? Give 'em the scoot if they stay too long."

"Got it." While most of Dottie's sayings seemed to be a tad off, that one felt spot on. "Speaking of guests, I've got tons to do to get ready. Especially with Sam being gone."

"Tulip!" Dottie yelled. "Get out here and say goodbye."

Tulip peeked around the corner. "Tell Sam that I have a present for him," she said before throwing out a half-hearted "Bye."

Dottie rolled her eyes. "Y'all have a merry Christmas over there," she said. "And thank you so much for the goodies."

Jessa stood to hug her. "Come back anytime you want."

Sam still wasn't home. She texted him again. *What time are your guests coming?* Maybe by texting him a direct question rather than a general one, he would be more likely to answer. She grabbed Fred's plate of cookies and made her way to her car. There still wasn't an answer when she neared the old gas station, and she was surprised to see the parking lot was packed with cars lining the road around it. It was just like kind-hearted Fred to be open on Christmas Eve.

The door chime announced her entry and there was Fred dressed in a red Santa suit with his beard once again colored white. If anyone wanted a photo, he was happy to oblige. She felt silly bringing a plate of cookies to a man surrounded by food. But it was the thought that counted, right? A woman ahead of her handed him a beautifully ribboned box. "Toffee," she said in a sweeter-than-candy voice, "my great-granny Fran's recipe." That had to be delicious. Fred came around and hugged her. "Thank you, Phyllis. That's mighty nice of you." The woman blushed all the way down past her low-cut blouse to her spiky red heels before reluctantly walking away.

Allie looked around as it dawned on her that most of the people in the store were women. Were they doing last-minute shopping, or had she accidentally thrown herself into a throng of single females vying for Fred's attention? She was twenty-three, and he had to be at least fifty. It was mortifying. Had he seen her? Maybe she could sneak out. She spun around and headed toward the door.

"Allie!" Fred yelled. "Come here!"

Damn. She'd been caught. She slinked her way to the front. "Hey, Fred. I brought you some cookies." She felt the eyes of the other women on her and wished she had the power to turn invisible.

"Thanks, hon. Dot said you'd be stopping by. Mighty neighborly of you."

Thank God he'd just made it clear that he saw it as neighborly, not flirty.

He pulled a bag from behind the counter and handed it to her. "This is for you, Sam, and Cuppie." He said it like they were a happy little family of three, and her heart swelled. She walked behind the counter and hugged him.

She pulled open the bag, and inside was a note that said FOR YOUR STOCKINGS. Did he know that she had actually hung some up? There were candy canes and card games and warm socks and dog treats. *He actually is Santa*, she thought as she climbed back into her car.

She turned into her driveway feeling more grateful than she'd felt in a long, long time. Her foot hit the brake when she saw a black official-looking car parked in front of her house. Sam's guests must have already arrived. Parking beside the vehicle, she peered through the darkened windows. No one was inside. Were they in the house? Sam's Jeep wasn't here, so he couldn't have let them in. Had she left the front door unlocked? She didn't think so. But evidence showed that someone was at her house, and it wasn't Sam.

He still hadn't answered her texts.

Chapter Nineteen

THE LIGHTS WERE off inside the cottage, and it was still and quiet. Yet Allie sensed someone was there. She was on high alert as she made her way to the kitchen and flipped on the light. A high-pitched "Oh!" made her jump, but it was followed by giggling laughter, directing her attention to the back porch.

On the rocking chairs were two figures, one male and one female, chatting animatedly. She'd recognize that curly blond bob hairstyle anywhere, because it had been her mother's for more than two decades. Allie froze. Her mother was here? She wasn't sure she was ready to see her. She'd only just now begun letting go of the anger. Her eyes shifted to the Christmas gifts underneath the tree. There was a pretty blue sweater wrapped in gold foil paper and a red bow. It had MAMA on the tag—physical evidence of Allie's hope.

Her mother had made the effort. She'd shown up. But just as soon as Allie was ready to run to the porch and hug her, the deep sound of a man's voice stopped her. What kind of woman was able to giggle and flirt when her husband lay cold in the ground? Plus, her mother knew darn well that

Allie didn't like surprises. Did she really think this would be welcome after almost an entire year of barely speaking? Allie leaned against the cold kitchen counter to keep steady, her eyes stuck on the two figures talking and laughing on her back porch. Where in the heck was Sam?

They hadn't seen her. She could sneak back out the front door and pretend like she'd never been there. It was approaching noon, so it would make perfect sense for her to drive to another island for lunch. Surely, something would be open on Christmas Eve. As she thought about it, she tiptoed to the front door, opening and closing it silently behind her. That's when her heart fell to her feet. A black BMW was coming up the drive. She'd forgotten to text Joey to cancel.

Even if she wanted to pretend like she remembered their date, she couldn't pull it off. Christmas Eve suppers were for velvet dresses and hostess gifts, and she was standing there empty-handed in jeans and a sweatshirt. There was no way to prepare for what was about to happen. No way to gracefully handle it.

The disappointed look on Joey's face was becoming too familiar. She ran up to his car like she was trying to stop an accident. He rolled down his window.

"I'm so sorry, Joey! My mama just showed up out of the blue, and I wasn't prepared."

His face softened, and he put the car in park. "Where's she in from?"

"Nashville." She moved aside so he could open the door and step out.

He was dressed in thick beige corduroys and a navy blue sweater, his dark hair parted on the side and slicked back. Without a word, he took her hand and led her up her own front stairs into the house. "What's your mother's name?" he asked.

"Susie." Her voice sounded small. "And I think her boyfriend's name is John." As soon as he grabbed her hand, she resigned herself to whatever was going to happen next. What choice did she have but to follow?

He went straight through the kitchen, saw them on the back porch, and opened the door. "Hey, y'all," he said. "I'm Joey."

The animated conversation they'd been having stopped, and the smile on her mother's face faded. She quickly shook Joey's hand, but her eyes were on Allie. "Oh, honey. I hope you don't mind that I'm here." What started as a soft, careful hug became tighter and tighter. "I've missed you so much," she said, her voice thick.

"I missed you too," Allie said, meaning it.

"I know you don't like surprises," she said into Allie's shoulder. "Please don't be mad."

"It's okay, Mama," she said, pulling away. "I'm glad you're here." That part was true. But it was equally true that she was unhappy her mother had brought along the gray-haired man currently talking to Joey like he was interviewing him for a job on Wall Street.

"And Joey is your boyfriend?" her mother asked with a smile.

"My coworker." As soon as the words were out of her mouth, Joey sidestepped closer and put his arm around her. Allie felt her face burn.

"Allie, this is John," her mother said, kindly ignoring the man's arm draped possessively across her daughter's shoulders. "I don't think you two have met yet."

"Hi," Allie said. "Merry Christmas." She didn't want to say *nice to meet you*, because it wasn't nice to meet him. Thankfully, the man didn't look like the type to hug her or force her into awkward unwanted conversation. He just smiled and said Merry Christmas back.

"How long are y'all here for?" Joey asked.

"A few days in Charleston, and then John rented us a place on Kiawah." Mama stuffed her hands into the fur-lined pockets of the same old black Patagonia jacket she'd had for as long as Allie could remember.

"It's cold," Allie said. "Please come inside."

"John, honey, would you mind getting the bags from the car?"

Allie cringed at the endearment. Were they planning to stay? There were only two bedrooms, and her old couch didn't pull out into a bed. Her mother must have seen her panic.

"Oh, no, we're not staying. I brought some things I

thought you might want from the storage unit."

What storage unit? she thought. "Mama? Did you move?" Was it even possible that her mother would leave another place without telling her?

"Of course not. Don't you remember? I went through that whole cleaning phase after your father died." She turned to Joey as if he should have full knowledge of her loss. "It was my therapy, it gave me something to put my mind to."

Now that she mentioned it, Allie did remember her mother's cleaning phase. She'd been busy with college graduation and looking for jobs, plus her apartment was in Midtown Nashville and her parents' house was in Brentwood, so she wasn't there every day. But she did recall her mother covered in paint and the house looking a little more refreshed and updated each time she came over.

John marched inside carrying two large shopping bags. Before he set them down next to Allie, her mother reached in and pulled out an old stuffed bear.

"Beary Bear!" Allie yelled, taking it gently from her mother and holding it to her chest. "I thought you threw him away!"

"I would never do that." Her mother reached inside the bag and placed trophies, yearbooks, even an old white jewelry box with a ballerina figurine on the kitchen counter. "I thought you might want these, but I'm keeping your baby clothes for when you give me a grandbaby."

"I thought all of this stuff was in a dump somewhere."

Allie was shocked at the intensity of the emotions it all brought up. Things she thought were gone forever were *back*. "I can't believe it."

"You thought I threw these treasures away?"

Allie nodded, her nose pressed against the bear.

"Why didn't you just ask me?" Her mother sighed and reached for John's hand. "Never mind. We don't need to go back there. I mean, I would like to keep moving forward if we can."

Allie nodded again. It was the first time she'd seen her mother look like she was in pain. Pain Allie had caused.

There was a ruckus outside the front door. The lock turned and Cuppie burst into the house. Allie was equal parts thrilled that they were okay and horrified about what they were walking in on. Sam was home, and Joey was currently meeting her only remaining parent. She immediately stepped away from him.

Cuppie ran to each person, sniffing them. When she got to John, she sat in front of him, staring up into his face, somehow still managing to wag furiously.

"Hey there, Buttercup," John said, stroking her head. "Good to see you again, old girl."

Sam came into the kitchen next. His face looked raw and his hair windblown. "Sorry I'm late, Colonel," he said, aggressively gripping palms with John.

Allie looked back and forth between them. They knew each other? "John is your commanding officer?" It was more of an observation than a question. "He's my mother's boyfriend."

Sam had a serious look on his face. "I was going to tell you."

"You knew?" She couldn't believe it. She turned to her mother. "And you aren't here to see me—you're here to see Sam?"

"Of course I'm here to see you." Her mother reached for her, but Allie jumped back.

"No." She felt a wildness take over her body. "No, you're not. You're here with them." She took several steps backward, bumping into Joey. She'd forgotten momentarily that he was in the room. She turned to face him. He was possibly the only person here who hadn't betrayed her. "I can't—" She couldn't get the words out.

"You can't stay here?" He filled in the words for her. "Or you can't leave with me?"

"I'm sorry," she said, then she turned on her heel and ran for the front door. She left it wide open as she sprinted down the front steps. The last thing she heard was Sam ordering Cuppie to follow her.

Chapter Twenty

EVEN THOUGH ALLIE had left so abruptly, it didn't feel like running away. It felt like self-care. She needed to push her body, inhale deeply, and reach and maintain a heart rate far above resting. She needed time alone to think. Cuppie stayed beside her, jogging along like she understood the assignment. They passed Dottie's house with its colorful Christmas bulbs, yellow truck in the driveway, and window cats. Then down the lane past someone's handmade Little Free Library, and on toward the bridge leading off the island. If she banked left before she got to it, there was a path to the ocean. As soon as she thought about it, she had to go. She might not have that ham and pickle sandwich for her dad that she'd planned on, but going to the beach was suddenly back on.

She wasn't ready to stop running, but the sand slowed her down, and the ocean had a calming effect that persuaded her to pause. As soon as she sat down, Cuppie leaned hard against her. Allie remembered how the dog had put her whole body between Sam and the overturned dresser. This felt like the same thing. "Are you trying to help me, Cup?"

Cuppie placed her furry face squarely against Allie's cheek.

"What happened today?" Allie asked as if Cuppie could answer. "Did you find the teenager?"

Of course Cuppie didn't answer. Everything she'd experienced as a military working dog, as a search-and-rescue dog, as Sam's dog, would be kept inside, never shared. Her yellow eyes stared straight ahead like the ocean held the answer to every question, like this giant wolf-dog had a connection to nature, and to the entire universe, that a human could never understand. A connection she shared by leaning her weight against Allie's side, by breathing, and by simply being there. Allie put her arm around the warm dog and turned her nose into her fur. "Thank you."

Something inside Allie broke—an emotional dam of sorts. She started talking to Cuppie and didn't stop until her fingers were blue and she could no longer feel her nose. She told her about how her dad was always busy at work. How providing for his family was his definition of being a good father, and because of that, she'd always craved more of him. He didn't know the name of her first boyfriend, what size shoe she wore, which best friend had unfairly turned on her, and which teacher said she wrote brilliant poetry.

She'd counted on the fact that one day her dad would retire. One day, he would slow down long enough to have time for her. One day, he might even need her or at least appreciate her. Now that day would never come. He'd died while she was off at college, and by then, he was too busy shutting down to be the father she needed. He'd been a shadow of himself, gaunt and gray, skinny as a bean pole, and desperately tired.

Then, Mark decided to move across the country. She was still in the worst pain of her life, and what did her boyfriend do? He left. She'd been abandoned by her father and her partner. How did a person overcome that? How did a person allow themselves to be vulnerable again? Where did they find the bravery to trust a man when the stakes were so high? A heart could only take a certain amount of damage before it was irrevocably broken.

Allie stared at the deep blue salt water along with Cuppie, watching the waves reach the shore and listening for the cadence. Nothing about the rhythm of the ocean was perfect. The waves didn't land on the correct foot each time, on the correct spot. They didn't avoid cracks in the sidewalk or tap the faucet three times before washing their hands. The waves freely did what they wanted. Some came in sideways, some large, some small, some curled, some flattened, but they all hit the shore just the same. And it was beautiful.

Allie breathed in deeply. She knew Sam. Knew him enough to trust, at least a little, that his intentions were good. So he'd invited his commanding officer, who happened to be her mother's boyfriend. Had he been trying to hurt her? No, absolutely not. Should she be willing to at least ask about his motivation? Ask why he'd done it? Probably.

Maybe what her mother needed was an invitation—even one extended by her daughter's roommate. Why was Allie so quick to think that everyone was against her? Especially the people who, in every other part of her life, seemed to be on her side. Why was she most angry with the people who genuinely cared about her? Maybe she wasn't being fair. It was Christmas Eve, and she'd just run out on a house full of people who cared about her. What was she doing subjecting poor Cuppie to the freezing beach when she should be curled up by the fire sound asleep?

Just as Allie went to stand, Cuppie jumped to full alert. She looked at Allie as if asking for permission, then barked several times and ran headlong into the ocean.

"Cuppie!" Allie yelled, panicked. "Cuppie, come back!" She'd left her phone back at the cottage, and the beach was completely empty. Even if she screamed as loud as she could for help, no one would hear her.

Cuppie knew to dive beneath the breaking waves, coming up for air in between until she made it past the break.

Allie pulled off her shoes and ran into the ocean up to her knees, yelling the dog's name. But Cuppie swam straight out into the depths—fast. That's when Allie caught sight of something dark and round in the distance, directly in the path of where Cuppie was headed. It was barely visible, and her eyes had trouble making out what it was, until she suddenly knew. Without a doubt. It was a person. *Oh my God.*

Allie was a good swimmer but not a great one. Plus, she was fully dressed. She walked farther out until the waves broke at her waist. The water was terribly cold. No one swam off the coast of South Carolina after October without a wetsuit.

"Hey!" she yelled at the faraway bobbing head, waving her arms. Cuppie was almost there. She watched as the dog grabbed hold of the person's collar with her teeth and began surging toward shore. As soon as she pulled the person close enough, Allie dove in and swam out to meet them. It was a young boy holding tight to a Camelbak water bladder he must've emptied and filled with air. He was on his back and didn't appear to be conscious except for the fact that he continued holding tight to the floating bag. Cuppie tugged on the boy's sweatshirt while Allie lifted his head higher out of the water so that it was easier for him to breathe. When they got to shore, she pulled beneath his shoulders until he was safely on the sand. Cuppie shook, then despite her tongue hanging long and tired, she took off running.

Please be getting Sam, Allie prayed. The boy was barely breathing. She knew she needed to warm him up, but she herself was soaked and freezing. The only thing she could think to do was pull him to her, shield him from the wind, and share whatever heat she had with his icy body. "You're safe now," she said softly and confidently. "We're getting help, and you're going to be warm very soon." He was curled like a baby in her arms, his head against her chest, and she found herself rocking him.

Hurry, Sam, she kept thinking. *Hurry.* "Hang in there, sweetheart, help is coming." She wore a tank top underneath her sweatshirt, so she pulled the heavy thing off, giving his cheek skin-to-skin access to her upper chest. She shook with the intense cold. Her sweatshirt was wet, but maybe it would still help hold in the heat, so she placed it on top of his head.

Hurry, Sam! She rocked the boy vigorously and sang to him the only song that she could think of. "We wish you a Merry Christmas, we wish you a Merry Christmas." *Please Sam, please hurry!* "Good tidings to you, and all of your kin."

Tears streaked down her face, and she allowed them to drop onto the boy's forehead. At least they were warm. They were the only warm thing between them. Her voice cracked as she tried to sing, "Good tidings for Christmas and a Happy New Year." She didn't know anything about hypothermia except for the fact that this boy had it, and that it was deadly.

Get here, Sam! Get here now!

Finally, the sound she'd been breathlessly anticipating came. Tires on gravel, a door opening, and Cuppie's bark. "Sam! Sam, run!" She did her best to yell, but her vocal cords felt frozen. Cuppie got there first, with Sam steps behind. She slumped with relief, somehow knowing that her mother and the colonel were there, too, but they were like apparitions in the fog of her brain. She felt a blanket placed around her shoulders and was lifted by a man and carried. Maybe the colonel? She wasn't sure. There were flashing lights, and she heard Sam's voice saying things like "BPM eighteen" and "temperature at 92.1." She heard a crinkling sound and caught a glimpse of a person wrapped in a silver blanket. She tried to speak, but it came out as a mumble. She wanted to ask if the boy was okay.

When her mind finally cleared, she was in Sam's Jeep with the heater blowing directly onto her. The colonel stood behind her mother, who was kneeling by the open passenger door, holding Allie's fingers up the vent. Sam was in the driver's seat, and the ambulance was gone. She was still shivering but could finally form the words "Is he okay?"

"If he makes it," Sam answered, "it's all thanks to you and Cup."

"It was Cuppie." Her lips still felt tight and cold.

"Says my frozen girl we found sitting on the beach singing Christmas carols and giving all of her warmth to that young man." Her mother spoke in a voice that held a certain softness—something like thankfulness, or maybe pride.

"Let's get her home," Sam said, his fingers gentle on her wrist. "Her pulse is strong, but she needs a hot bath."

"Cuppie too," Allie added.

"Cuppie too," Sam agreed.

"I bought stuff for charcuterie," Allie said as they neared the house. "And for dinner."

"I'll handle all of that," her mother said. "After I give you a bath."

Allie felt herself smile. "You're going to give me a bath, Mama?"

"I'm going to sit there with you and make sure you're safe. Just like I used to."

"Thank you," Allie said, wrapping her stiff fingers around her mother's hand. "Thank you for being here."

Chapter Twenty-One

ALLIE'S LIPS WERE pink again, her body warmed deep into the core for more reasons than just the bath, the hot cocoa, and her seat closest to the fire. Mama was busy cooking in the kitchen and a plate of salami, cheese, grapes, nuts, honey, crackers, and chocolate was beautifully arranged on a red Christmas platter and set on the coffee table. John was hunched over the kitchen counter chopping vegetables next to her mother, something Allie's father never did, and Sam was sound asleep on the couch with Cuppie, who snored softly.

Allie had on her softest sweatshirt and fuzzy socks, her hair freshly washed and dried, when she snuck her way into the middle of the sleeping pile on the couch. Sam lifted his arm and welcomed her in.

"You know what I realized on the beach today?" she whispered.

"Hmm?"

"You and I might seem really different, but Cuppie deals with us in the same way."

"She knows stuff." He chuckled, his eyes still closed.

"Are you actually awake? Or do you need to sleep more?"

"I'm awake if you're ready to talk," he said, stretching.

"How long have you known that John's girlfriend is my mom?" Her voice held no anger. She just genuinely wanted to know.

He pulled himself into a sitting position, and she did the same. Cuppie gave them both a look of annoyance for waking her up. "Can I hold your hands while I tell you this?" Sam asked. "I really need for you to believe me."

She turned and offered her hands to him.

"John was the person who told me about Goose Island."

Allie's eyes went to the man in the kitchen working alongside her mother. "Wait a minute. Have you met my mother before?"

He nodded.

She started to pull her hand away, but he held tighter. "So"—she started to put the pieces together—"did you know who I was when you moved in?"

"I didn't know it was you when I signed the lease. I only knew your mother as Susie and you as Allie. The name on your lease said Allison."

She tugged her hand away from him. "Wait a minute. You're on Goose Island because John told you what? That there was a single girl out here living alone?"

"That's not what happened at all. Yes, I figured it out pretty fast. But, no, I didn't move here for you. I moved here for me and for Cuppie. We'd been searching for a place just like this: a small town near the water with neighbors who cared enough to know our names. I didn't come here looking for a girlfriend. I didn't even want a girlfriend."

Allie noticed that the kitchen was suddenly empty. Her mother and John must've recognized the tone of the conversation and made themselves scarce.

"Here's what I know," he went on. "I've met a lot of people. I've dated plenty. Too many, probably. I've looked around enough, and I've never met someone like you. Ever. And yes, I knew things about you before I met you. I knew that you'd just been through some terrible losses. I knew that you were independent and smart and hardworking. I knew that you were beautiful." He rubbed his hand through his short hair. "Look, I would never purposefully move in with someone I thought I might be interested in dating. That would be stupid."

She relaxed. He was right. Moving in with someone you hoped to date would be a sure-fire recipe for disaster. She exhaled and placed her hand palm up on his knee. He took it, and his little grin was back.

"I'm pushing for my house to be finished as soon as possible," he said. "There's plenty of room for you there. But it will be your choice, okay? When the time comes."

She nodded, a tingly feeling of relief flowing through her. He had room in his house for her?

"For now, though, I would really like to try this, here, with you."

"Try what?" She smirked. "You're gonna try me on and if I don't fit, you'll return me? Am I your new Christmas sweater?"

"You know that's not what I'm saying."

She did know. The whole reason for dating was to try a person on and see if they fit. But she needed him to be clear.

"I don't want to be a secret anymore, and I don't want you to see Joey," he said plainly. "I don't want you to go out with anyone but me."

"And who will you be going out with?" She scoffed. If they were going to date each other, she wanted a commitment.

"Just you, ya dingbat." He laughed and tried to kiss her, but she giggled and pushed him away.

"Dingbat, huh? Well, this dingbat likes to ensure that both parties are on the same page before she makes life-altering decisions."

"Yes, ma'am," he said. "I hear you loud and clear." He slipped off the couch and got down on one knee. Taking her other hand, he said, "Allie Westley, will you please be my girlfriend?" His eyes twinkled and she thought her heart might jump from her chest. "To clarify," he said, "that means that I will be the sole owner of the title *Allie's boyfriend*, and I am free to call myself that in public to everyone. You will not have romantic relationships with any other people, especially people named Joey. I will also commit to kissing only you and having romantic feelings only toward you. I'll do my best to meet your wants and needs, I will treat you as my respected partner, and...what else?"

"Well, if we're making a list, I like foot rubs."

"I will occasionally rub your feet," he added, taking his seat on the hearth. "But only when they're not stinky."

"That's fair." She pretended to contemplate further. "And you will not enter my room when the door is locked."

"Of course. Unless you yell for help, in which case, I will break that damned door down."

"Yes, I accept that term."

"And you will make your mama's cookies at Christmas," he said.

"Yes, I will. And I'll keep milk on hand to go with them."

The back porch door opened, and her mother and John walked in. "It's cold out there," Susie said. "Sorry, y'all, we were trying to give you some privacy, but I couldn't make it any longer. Plus, I've got to get the roast in the oven."

"Mama, John," Allie said, squeezing Sam's hands. "I'd like to introduce you to my boyfriend, Sam."

CHRISTMAS MORNING, ALLIE and Sam ate cinnamon rolls and opened presents. Thanks to Fred, there was something in each of their stockings. And thanks to her mother, Allie's old stuffed bear peeked out from the top of hers. She wrapped a bottle of her best wine and tied a ribbon around the neck for John. Her mother seemed happy with him, and why would Allie wish unhappiness on anyone? Maybe it was just that simple. A new love didn't mean the old love was diminished. Her mother could love her dad and still have room to love John. If it was true that there would never be the same love twice, what was wrong with allowing a new love in?

Sam was wearing a new black beanie Tulip had knitted just for him, and Cuppie chewed noisily on her new beef bone by the fire when the news broke in on the televised Christmas Day parade. The young man who had been rescued on Christmas Eve after a fishing trip gone wrong was recovering in a local hospital. Paul Easton, fifteen, had been fishing for sheepshead from the rocks when a rogue wave pulled him in. Using his Boy Scout survival knowledge, he inflated the Camelbak water bladder he wore like a backpack and used it as a flotation device. Searchers had been working round the clock in shifts, but it was a Goose Island local and her dog who rescued him from the water.

Happiness enveloped Allie like a warm blanket. "I can't believe his name is Paul Easton," she said, squeezing Sam's knee a little too hard. "My dad's name is Paul Westley. Am I the only one who thinks that's strange?"

Sam, in his plaid pajama bottoms and red GINGERBREAD HOUSE CONSTRUCTION TEAM T-shirt, stopped before putting a bite of cinnamon roll in his mouth. "Dottie would say it's a sign."

"Dottie would say that God switched the flip on the names," Allie laughed. The woman couldn't get a phrase right if her life depended on it.

Susie and John were coming back by that day, and Allie invited everyone for ham and pickle sandwiches on the beach. She could hardly wait. Now that she had family again, she wasn't as pent-up and anxious. She hadn't even tapped her toe on the line between the carpet and the hardwood as she left her bedroom that morning. She felt giddy as she recognized that her compulsions were beginning to relax. Thank God. It was up and down with them depending on what was happening in her life, so she knew to appreciate the reprieve. She stared at the Christmas tree, and an overwhelming sense of peace overtook her. The lights blurred together.

Merry Christmas, Dad.

There was a moment of darkness, then the lights came back on.

"Did you see that?" Sam asked. "I think we lost power for a second."

She leaned into him, resting her head on his shoulder. "No need to check the breaker," she said. "Everything's fine."

"Maybe it was Santa landing on the roof," he said. "One of his reindeer stepped on a power line."

"You know what?" she said, unwrapping a candy cane.

"It was definitely Santa. I am absolutely positive that he exists. As a matter of fact, it had to be Santa who messed up my rental application by magically making me click *male* instead of *female*."

"Ah," Sam scoffed. "So, it was you. The truth finally comes out."

"No, it wasn't me. It was *Santa*." She giggled. "The truth shall help you see." Allie did her best Dottie impression with a candy cane poking out of her mouth.

"I think the saying is, the truth shall set you free," Sam corrected.

"The truth shall be the key," she declared, giggling.

"The truth is where I want to be." His voice lowered as he moved the candy cane from her mouth and his lips near hers. "The truth is you and me." He kissed her sweetly. "Merry Christmas, Allie."

"Merry Christmas, Sam."

The End

More Books by Laurie Beach

Book 1: *The Firefly Jar*

Book 2: *Blink Twice If You Love Me*

Book 3: *Christmas in Crickley Creek*

Available now at your favorite online retailer!

About the Author

Photographer: Stephanie Lynn Co

Laurie Beach writes about small southern beach towns, quirky friendships, and true love. When she's not holding down the couch and typing out words, she stays busy keeping track of her husband and four children. A graduate of Auburn University with degrees in Mass Communications and Psychology, she worked as a television news reporter, an advertising producer, and a political press secretary. She now writes full-time.

Thank you for reading

A Saltwater Christmas

If you enjoyed this book, you can find more from all our great authors at TulePublishing.com, or from your favorite online retailer.